Raised as a Goon 3

Lock Down Publications and Ca$h

Presents

Raised as a Goon 3

A Novel by *Ghost*

Lock Down Publications
P.O. Box 1482
Pine Lake, Ga 30072-1482

Copyright 2017 by Ghost Raised as a Goon 3

All rights reserved. No part of this book may be reproduced in any form or by electronic or mechanical means, including information storage and retrieval systems without permission in writing from the publisher, except by a reviewer who may quote brief passages in review.
First Edition October 2017
Printed in the United States of America

This is a work of fiction. Names, characters, places, and incidents either are products of the author's imagination or are used fictitiously. Any similarity to actual events or locales or persons, living or dead, is entirely coincidental.

Lock Down Publications
Like our page on Facebook: Lock Down Publications
@
www.facebook.com/lockdownpublications.ldp
Cover design and layout by: **Dynasty Cover Me**
Book interior design by: **Shawn Walker**
Edited by**: Mia Rucker**

Stay Connected with Us!

Text **LOCKDOWN** to 22828 to stay up-to-date with new releases, sneak peaks, contests and more…

Thank you!

Submission Guideline.

Submit the first three chapters of your completed manuscript to ldpsubmissions@gmail.com, subject line: Your book's title. The manuscript must be in a .doc file and sent as an attachment. Document should be in Times New Roman, double spaced and in size 12 font. Also, provide your synopsis and full contact information. If sending multiple submissions, they must each be in a separate email.

Have a story but no way to send it electronically? You can still submit to LDP/Ca$h Presents. Send in the first three chapters, written or typed, of your completed manuscript to:

LDP: Submissions Dept
Po Box 1482
Pine Lake, Ga 30072

DO NOT send original manuscript. Must be a duplicate.

Provide your synopsis and a cover letter containing your full contact information.

Thanks for considering LDP and Ca$h Presents.

Dedications

This book is dedicated to my precious baby girl 3/10. I love you more than anything and everything in this world. You're the reason why I'm putting the birds down and trying to find another way. You deserve the best possible future.

Acknowledgements

Mad love to whole LDP family. We got this!

Note to readers

I sincerely appreciate all love and support of this project. Thank you for giving me a fair chance. Please believe that my best it yet to come. My works are raw and uncut, never expect them to be anything less than real. I'll always give it to you how I remember it. This is me.

Chapter 1

My father tightened his grip on my mother's neck and slammed her more aggressively into the wall. "You tryin' to take over my family, and you fuckin' my wife! I promise you this gon' be a night that you never forget!"

Juice held up both of his twin .40 calibers. One was pointed at me and the other was pointed at Princess. He had a look on his face that said he was ready to body me and her. "I'm gon' enjoy this shit." he said through clenched teeth.

I curled my lip, walking further into the living room. "Fuck you niggas. What, we s'pose to bow down cause y'all got guns out?" I spit on the carpet. "This shit ain't got nothin' to do wit my mother. Everything that she did was because I was runnin' the show while you was on lock, pops, so if you wanna take that shit out on anybody, take it out on me. I'm a man, and I can handle it. Y'all can let these women go." I waved my hand toward my sister, Princess, and my mother. I was already thinking about my lil' daughter sleeping in the other room. I knew that my father and brother didn't give a fuck about hurting nobody, including a baby.

"Nigga, fuck you! You ain't nothin' but a snake. First, you get me locked up so you can fuck my bitch. Then, at the same time, you got our mother crawlin' in the bed wit you. I should pop you in yo muthafuckin' head right now."

"Fuck you, Juice! And I ain't yo bitch. I never belonged to you. We only fucked twice, and I was not impressed. Taurus is my nigga. And if you even think about killin' him, then you might as well kill me too, or else I'm comin' fa yo head. That's on our daughter. You already kilt my brother and ain't shit happen to you, yet. I'll be damned if you think you finna kill the love of my life, and walk away from that shit unscathed."

"Bitch, shut up. And fuck yo stupid ass brother. That nigga ain't deserve to live no mo'. I kilt that nigga and ain't feel shit. Spent his portion of the money, too. The first time I fucked you at the Ramada Inn, I paid the bill with his cut of that lick. Ain't nothin' like fuckin' a nigga sister after you kill his ass. That made the pussy feel so much better." He laughed out loud.

Princess ran at him. When she got within arm's length, he smacked her so hard that she fell to the floor, and was knocked out cold. I ran up on that nigga and he pointed both guns at me, stopping me in my tracks.

"Come on, bitch nigga. You wanna play Captain Save a Hoe, I'mma knock yo head off, and every other muthafucka head in here, besides my old man's. I'm tide of yo shit anyway. The only reason I ain't bodied you yet, is 'cuz pops ain't gave me the go ahead. But try me, and I'mma have to take the ass whoopin' he gon' hand down for goin' against his wishes. You gon' be a dead nigga. Word is bond."

I knelt down and picked Princess' head up into my arms. I could see a speckle of blood in the corner of her mouth. Just seeing it had my heart beating fast. I wanted to kill that nigga, Juice. I didn't give a fuck if he was my brother or not.

I heard my mother gag. I looked up to see my father squeezing her neck. "Bitch, you know better. You out here fuckin' our son while I was in that muthafucka tryna get our lives on track. What type of shit is that?"

Her face was turning redder and redder. "Please, baby. Please, let me go. I promise I won't do it again. I was just lonely, and I needed him. He the only one that love me. I-" She gagged.

He tightened his grip. "Bitch, he the only one that love you? How the fuck you figure that when I been puttin' up wit yo country ass ever since you was fourteen years old. I'm the one that been feedin' this family and makin' sure we all stayed above water. He ain't did ten percent of what I've been doin', even before he was born. So, tell me how the hell he love you more than I do." He got into her face so close that his forehead was against hers. "Speak!"

When he let her throat go a little bit, she exhaled loudly. She coughed for a few seconds. "Baby, I'm just sorry. Please, let's forget about this. I promise I'll do anything. All you have to do is name it." Tears sailed down her cheeks.

"Oh, I know. You definitely gonna do that. But for right now, we gon' take care of your part-time lover." He spat the words nastily. "I can't believe you. You could have at least turned to our oldest son. Nall, you skipped him for that dead nigga right there." He dropped her to the floor, and stood over me, placing the barrel of his gun to my forehead. "I should blow yo muthafuckin' head off right here, you turncoat. How the fuck you gon' betray this family like that?"

Princess began to stir in my arms, finally awaking from her slumber. When her eyes opened, she saw that my father was holding the gun to my head, and her eyes got bucked. "On some real shit, pops, you can let these women go. Me, you and, Juice can handle this shit like men. This ain't got nothin' to do wit them."

I clenched my jaw. I was heated and ready for whatever that was going to happen to take place because I wasn't feeling how they was trying to treat me. I was ready for the bullets.

As long as I knew that the women in my family weren't going be harmed, I was good. I was supposed to be their sacrifice.

My father pressed the barrel even harder to my forehead and bit into his bottom lip. Lil' nigga, you really think you runnin' the show now, huh? You think just 'cuz you make a few moves with a fuckin' Russian and Hood Rich n'em out in the Windy City, that you on my level, and that it means you can take over my family? That you supposed to sit on my throne of this castle? Huh?"

I swallowed, as I felt the tear sail down my cheek. "All I'm sayin' is that preyin' on women is bitch shit. You got a problem wit me, y'all can let them go, and y'all can do whatever to me. That's man shit." I looked toward my mother. "Excuse my language, too, ma."

She smiled and nodded. "It's okay, baby."

My father laughed. "This shit ain't real. You two muhfuckas flirtin' right in front of me." He shook his head. "I'll tell you what we gon' do. Juice, you finna whoop his ass until he can't get up. I mean, I want you to fuck him up. Teach this bitch a lesson since he wanna be they sacrifice." He looked down to me. "You think you ready to take my throne. Well, first you gon' have to go through my first born. You whoop him, and we'll see where shit goes."

"Please, no, daddy," Mary whined. "I don't wanna see them fight. We're supposed to be a family."

He grabbed her by her hair roughly and kissed her on the lips briefly. "Shut up, baby girl, and stay in a child's place. This is grown folks' business." He threw her to the floor. "Now everybody out. Let's go into the backyard where these two gonna fight to the death. And the death is what I mean 'cuz we ain't leavin' from back there 'til one of you need to be buried."

I helped Princess get to her feet. She stood on wobbly legs, leaning against me as we made our way to the backyard. "Baby, you better whoop his ass, too. I mean, fuck him up. That nigga can't fuck wit yo business. Never could, and never will be able to. Any man that put his hands on a female ain't nothin', but a bitch nigga."

"Bitch, shut up. I'm finna whoop this nigga, and then I'mma whoop yo ass next. All that shit you talkin' about a nigga being a bitch if he hit a female, well watch me whoop this nigga right after I get done knockin' yo ass clean out." he laughed.

"Fuck you, Juice!" Princess spat.

"Nah, we already did that. You ain't got enough meat on yo bones for me. I mean what good is it bein' in the south if niggas running around fuckin' yo skinny ass. This is the land of thick bitches. You s'pose to be in Cali somewhere with the rest of them starvin' hoes."

I saw another tear drop from Princess' eye. "I swear, if I was a man I'd whoop yo ass myself. I'd fight you to the death and shit on yo corpse. You ain't worth the life that Jehovah gave you."

"Allah gave me life. Jehovah ain't gave me shit," he said, taking off his shirt and revealing his ripped-up body.

"Baby, be cool. Don't keep goin' back and forth with him. You are a Queen. And you're beyond beautiful, just like our daughter that mirrors you."

She nodded her head. "Thank you, baby."

"Alright, enough wit all that sappy shit. Let's get the show on the road. Since you think you man enough to run this family, and you wanna over step yo brother to sit on this throne, I wanna see you go through him. Prove to me that you're worthy, and he's not."

I put Princess behind me, and led her all the way to the picket fence that was around our backyard. "Listen, no matter what, you stay right here. I mean that. Win, lose, or draw. I don't want you to move from this fence. You gotta keep our daughter in mind now, no matter what happens to me." I rubbed her soft cheek. "Do you understand that?"

She shook her head. "Fuck that, Taurus. I don't want to be on this earth if you ain't on it. I love you ten times more than our daughter. I would never be able to raise her without you in the picture. Word is bond, if they kill you then they better kill me next because I don't want to be here without you. I just can't."

I knew how she felt. To me it was pointless to try and talk any sense into her because, knowing her the way that I did, her mind was made up. And as crazy as it may sound, I respected her decision. I just felt I couldn't lose, even though I knew my brother was a beast wit his hands.

She kissed me on the lips. "Do yo thang, daddy. Do it for me and know that I love you to the death."

I curled my upper lip, and nodded. "I love you, too, lil' mama." As soon as I turned around to face that nigga Juice, he swung, punching me so hard in the jaw that I saw blue lightening. I got dizzy immediately. That nigga hit hard.

"Let's go, bitch nigga!" He swung, punching me in the ribs, damn near knocking the wind out of me.

I ran a little bit to gather myself. Once I got a safe enough distance away, I cleared my head by taking a deep breath, and then I put my guards up. He ain't waste no time rushing me, and swinging at the same time. I waited for him to get close. He swung with a right cross. I ducked and came up with a left hook that crashed right into his earlobe. *Bam*!

He hollered, "Ahhhh, you bitch nigga. I'mma kill you!" He rushed me at full speed, this time more calculating with his attack. He threw up his guard, protecting his chin.

I slowly made my way back toward him. I threw a jab that he blocked, and followed that with a right cross that caught him in the cheek. He threw another jab that busted my lips, and then a left hook that caught me in my right eye, knocking me backward.

"Yeah, I see I gotta be smart wit yo ass. I'm finna kill you, nigga." He threw a bunch of punches to my body, fucking me up. Then he tried to uppercut me to finish me off, but I blocked it, punching him in the same ear again. *Bam*! "Ahh, you muthafucka."

I took that lil' distraction to kick him straight in the nuts. As soon as he bent over to protect them, I scooped him, dumping him on his back. He hollered out in pain.

"Get 'em, daddy. Kill that nigga. Kill 'em. Please!" Princess yelled with her back to the fence.

He struggled to get to his feet, but halfway there, I scooped him again and dumped him on his back with so much venom that he bounced off the ground like a basketball.

"Get yo punk ass up and fight, Juice! All that dope you been doin' done turnt you into a straight bitch!" I kicked him in the ribs and he flipped onto his back, groaning in pain.

"Fuck this fightin' shit, pops, shoot that nigga. Shoot this nigga dead!" he hollered in the direction of our father.

I kicked him in the ribs again. "Treat me like a lady, nigga. You so quick to fight these females. Well pretend I'm one. Come on." I backed up so he could get to his feet and, boy, why did I do that?

My father pushed me on the back and Juice caught me with two haymakers right in my chest and mouth, knocking me to the ground. Then my father kicked me in the back, and Juice kicked me in the shoulder. I was dizzy, and felt like I wanted to throw up.

"Yeah, it ain't no fun when the rabbit got the gun, huh?"

He picked me up by the head, scooped me into the air, and fell backwards with me. I landed on my back and bounced off the ground with the wind knocked out of me and blood coming out of my nose.

Princess ran from the gate and punched Juice so hard that he fell to one knee in a daze. Then she kicked my father in the nuts and jumped on top of him, punching him again and again until he threw her off him.

"You stupid bitch." He ran, picked her up by her neck, and slammed her to the ground, straddling her and smacking her again and again. "Bitches are made to be beaten," he kept repeating as he slapped her repeatedly.

I elbowed Juice in his face, causing blood to spurt everywhere. He tackled me and bit me on the shoulder, causing so much pain that I hollered out like a bitch. He had the nerve to pick a different spot and bite me again, causing equal pain as before.

I elbowed him in the back of the head three times until he let me go, and then I slapped the shit out of him, making him do a 180, before I jumped on his back, grabbed a hand full of his dreads, and slammed his face into the grass again and again until he became unconscious. Then I got up and ran full speed at my father, who was ripping Princess' blouse down the middle, looking like he was getting ready to rape her.

"Yeah, you lil' bitch. Since you think you so muthafuckin' tough, let's see how you handle me stickin' this big ass dick up yo ass and fuckin' you until you bleed," he growled, right before I tackled his ass.

But it seemed like he was ready for that because, as soon as I tackled him, we tussled on the ground for a hot second before he came up with his gold .45 pressed to my temple and Juice's gun aimed at Princess, who had picked up a big ass brick ready to bash his shit in.

"Now both of you muthafuckas hold on a minute, right now. This ain't finna go down like that." He stood up, rolling his head around his neck. Looking over at Juice, he shook his head, eyeing me and Princess closely. "Y'all done fucked my son up, and put ya hands on me. Now, somethin' has got to give."

Princess lowered her eyes into slits. "Drop that gun, ol' man, and fight us like the gangsta you frontin' to be. We ain't got no guns, and yet we fuckin' y'all up," she snickered, licking her juicy lips.

"Lil' girl, I see you just gotta death wish, don't you?" He cocked the hammer back on Juice's gun and turned it sideways.

Princess smiled. "Do what you gonna do, 'cuz I ain't scared of you, or no other father walkin' this earth. You can only kill me, after that, you ain't got nothin' on me. So, fuck death, and fuck you, too. Y'all touched my man, so one way or the other, you gon' have to kill me anyway."

We heard crying that caught our attention, and we all looked toward the back door of the house just in time to see about fifty niggas with red rags around their necks filing into the backyard. They had a female in front with a red bandana halfway across her face holding Jahliya, and she was throwing a fit.

Princess started to run toward her, but was caught like a deer in headlights as the masked men drew their guns, aiming them at us. I thought shit like this only happened on television. My father laughed.

"Now that's the shit I'm talking about right there. Bring me my grandbaby, my daughter, and my wife."

The female did as she was told. My father planted a kiss on my daughter's forehead. My sister, Mary and my mother were thrown at his feet violently, both with tears and the look of fear in their eyes.

"You know, Taurus, women are the essential foundation of any family, includin' ours. If you conquer the woman, you conquer the entire household." He frowned and then looked down, first at my daughter, then at my mother and Mary. "For now, I won them, your daughter included. I will tell you when you can have your daughter back. For now, you have left a real nasty taste in my mouth, and until I figure out how to get rid of it, I'm gon' possess these females, and that includes your little girl." He leaned down, kissed her on the forehead, and smiled at her. "She so pretty. Look just like her grand-daddy."

"Quit puttin' yo nasty ass lips on my baby. She don't belong to you," Princess snapped. "Just give her to us and leave our family alone."

The woman with the red bandana across her face, pulled out a long-ridged knife that gleamed in the night. "Just give me the word, pop, and I'll cut this bitch's throat out."

Princess damn near broke her neck to look at the woman. "Bitch, who is you talkin' about?" she asked, walking over to her without taking her eyes away from her.

I grabbed her by the arm, pulling her back to me. "That a be stupid, baby."

"Fuck that, I don't even know this bitch and she makin' it seem like she gonna do somethin' to me. Well bring it, bitch. I ain't got nothin' to lose. You muthafuckas done took my daughter and assaulted my man. What do I have to lose, huh?"

I wrapped her in my arms with her back to my chest. "It's gon' be alright, baby. Trust me."

My father laughed. "Yeah, trust him." He shook his head. "Y'all snatch up these women of my bloodline, and let's get up outta here before I kill somebody."

I watched as they snatched up my mother and Mary, and surrounded my father, giving him all the protection that he needed, while their guns remained aimed at us.

"Don't worry, Taurus, you'll get this little girl back when I feel like it's time for you to have her."

"That's if I don't kill her first," Juice chimed in, getting helped up from the ground by three of the Bloodz. "You gon' pay for this day. I can promise you that."

My father shrugged his shoulders. "Yeah, I guess if he don't kill her first." He walked out of the backyard with my daughter in his arms.

Chapter 2

Every time me and Princess needed to think deeply we wound up at the lakefront, sitting on the big rocks, overlooking the water as it crashed into the boulders. The sun was just coming up. The air was thick with moisture. I could already tell that it was going to be a sweltering day.

Princess got up and climbed down the big rocks, making her way back to the parking lot. She nearly fell twice trying to climb down them. The whole time we had been at the lake-front she had not uttered a word. Now I was curious as to where she was going. I got up to follow behind her.

"Princess, where are you goin'?" I asked, trying to catch up to her. I had to be careful because the rocks were slick with dew, and the Jordans I had on my feet had poor grips on the bottom of them.

Princess got back to my truck, tried to open the door twice, and failed. Then she kicked the side of it, and slid down to her butt with her hands covering her face. "This is some bullshit! What type of life am I livin' where I lose my brother and my daughter to the same muthafuckas? What is life?" she screamed, as she broke down crying.

I knelt beside her and tried to place my hand on her shoul-der to console her but she smacked it away. "What's good ma?"

She jumped to her feet. "Nall, fuck you, too, Taurus. Fuck you and those evil ass people!" she screamed at the top of her lungs and then took off into a sprint across the parking lot.

I chased right behind her until I caught up with her. Grab-bing her and wrapping my arms around her, I said, "Baby, you freakin' out like this, ain't gone get our daughter back, especially if you takin' this shit out on me. We supposed to be in this thing together." I held her closer to me and kissed her on the forehead.

She laid her head on my chest and cried her little heart out, figuratively. I felt her body shaking, and that caused tears to come into my eyes. Very slowly, everything that we were going through started to take a toll on me. The more she cried in my arms, the more it hit home.

It felt like she was calming down, and then out of the blue she took a step back and pushed me so hard that I damn near busted my shit. "How could you just let him take our daughter away? How could you let him almost rape me? You're supposed to be my protector, but look at all that happened. I hate you!" She smacked me across the face, and took off running toward the water. "Fuck this life! I can't take it anymore."

I had to shake the cobwebs out of my head, and then I was running in big strides right behind her, trying to stop her from jumping into the water, but it was too late. As soon as she got to the big rocks, she climbed them like a professional. The next thing I knew, she was jumping into the water head first. I remembered her telling me that she had never learned how to swim, so she was basically on the verge of committing suicide. She made a big splash into the water, came up for a second, and then sank back down.

I ran at full speed, climbed the rocks, and dived in right after her, landing next to her. By that time, her body was calm and it seemed like she was trying to drown herself because as I opened my eyes under the water, I could see that she had her mouth wide open, and blood was coming from her nose. I grabbed her and pulled her to the surface.

As soon as our heads came above water, she inhaled a huge gust of air, and then started to punch at me. “Let me go! I can’t take this shit no more!” She scratched me across the face, and I let her go. She tried to sink back into the water, and I pulled her up again. The water was freezing cold, and it was starting to take my breath away. When I felt her bite into my arm, I let her go again. Once more she tried to sink to the bottom. That time, when I pulled her up, I smacked the shit out of her, making her yelp.

“Now stop this stupid shit, Princess! Get yo ass out this water and we gon’ figure out how to get our daughter back. Right now, you breakin’ down on me.”

She nodded, water going into her face and up her nose. “Okay, daddy. Okay, I’m sorry. I just lost myself for a minute. Let’s get out of here.” She allowed me to lead us to shore.

“Hey, leave her alone. I’m calling the police on you, asshole,” said a big white dude with long surfer’s hair.

I was so muthafucking mad that I couldn’t wait to get to shore to get on his ass. I started to swim as hard as I could until we made it onto the sand. As soon as we did, I bounced up and ran full speed until I tackled his white ass like I played for the Chicago Bears. I mean, I picked him up in the air and must’ve carried him about twenty feet before I slammed him to the ground on his back.

“Punk ass white man. Mind yo own muthafuckin’ business,” I hollered, and kicked him in the ribs.

“Fuck you, you psycho nigger!” He jumped up and tackled me to the ground, and we started wrestling. I couldn’t even lie, that white dude was strong as a muthafucka. He kept trying to take my head and slam it into the pavement, but I wouldn’t let him. Finally, I kneed him in the nuts and he let a loud, "Ohhh," before rolling to his side with his hands between his legs.

"Bitch mafucka! That's what you get." I kicked him in the ribs, and started stomping him so hard that I nearly fell, more than once. I was angry and I felt like he was the perfect person to take my anger out on. I imagined that he was Serge, Nastia's father, that had put me through so much shit that it nearly drove me crazy.

"Hey, you get off him. I'm calling the police!" some white lady yelled from the parking lot. She looked like she had been jogging. She was dressed in some tight biker shorts and a sport's bra. I noted that she had headphones on her head that were connected to her phone.

I looked down at the white dude who was crying, trying to catch his breath with his arms wrapped around his ribs.

"You fucking broke my ribs, man. What's your problem?"

I stomped him again, and he hollered. "Shut the fuck up! Shut up." I demanded, and thought about chasing the white girl down before she called the police.

She took her phone and seemed to be dialing the number to law enforcement when Princess ran up on her and snatched the phone out of her hands. "I hate snitches, bitch," she said, and then punched her square in the nose. She then picked her up and slammed her to the concrete while the woman screamed at the top of her lungs.

"Get that bitch, baby. Take all yo anger out on her ass!" I didn't know why I was advising her to make such a stupid decision, but in that moment, all I thought about was death.

I leaned down and straddled the white dude. Grabbing his head into my hands, I took it and slammed it backward into the concrete, sending it ricocheting off the ground. Blood splattered under it immediately, and it got me excited. I started to think about my daughter, and the next thing I knew, I was slamming his head into the concrete until I felt the back of it becoming mush.

I saw Princess dragging the white girl by her hair across the parking lot. She had her by the back of my truck, then she popped open the back of it, took out the crow bar, and closed it back. Before I could figure out what she had on her mind, she brought the crow bar down on to the woman's face at full speed, connecting with her skull and causing blood to splatter all over the place. She raised it above her head again and brought it back down, this time so hard that it got stuck inside of the blonde's head. She had to place her wedge sandals on to the side of the woman's face to pry it out. Then she brought it down again and again. She looked like a little kid destroying a pumpkin.

The man under me didn't move. I laid my head on his chest to see if there was a heartbeat, but I couldn't hear one. I shrugged my shoulders and slammed the back of his head into the concrete again, and then stood up. "Baby, let's go," I yelled as Princess slammed the iron into the side of the woman's head and left it there.

"What?" she hollered, prying the crow bar out of the woman's temple and standing up with blood all over her shirt. She pointed to her ear. "I can't hear you."

I waved. "I said let's go before somebody show up!"

She nodded and wiped the crow bar on the woman's Sport's bra. She jumped into the driver's seat of my truck, started it up, and drove to me. I jumped in and she peeled away.

I noted that she was breathing incredibly hard when I got into the car. "Damn, don't tell me my baby girl all out of shape and shit. You lookin' like all you do is smoke cigarettes or somethin'," I laughed, still thinking about my daughter but trying to steer the subject in another direction.

"Nall, I'm good. I had to fuck that bitch up, though. You already know I hate snitches. I already lost my daughter today. I ain't tryna have that bitch get my baby daddy taken away just because she wanna be a good Samaritan. I got her phone, too." She threw it on my lap.

I frowned. "For what? We don't need this bitch shit."

She sucked her teeth. "I know. But while I was strugglin' wit her, I touched it more than once. My fingerprints all over that mafucka so I had to bring it wit me. I got that and the crow bar."

I saw blood all over her cheeks, and face. I took my shirt off and started to wipe her face off. "Damn, baby, what made you introduce her ass to that crow bar, though. I mean, you fucked her up."

"On some real shit, I got to imaginin' that that bitch was yo father. Once I allowed myself to imagine that, it was all over."

"Me too," I said letting my seat all the way back.

"You too what?" she asked, pulling up to a red light, and turning in her seat to look at me.

"I imagined that that white dude was my father and Juice, and before I knew it, I was killin' his ass in cold blood and not givin' a fuck. Them takin' our daughter was the wrong thing for them to do, you know that right?"

She curled her upper lip. "You know we gotta find they ass and kill 'em. And I mean kill 'em so cold that a mafucka never think about fuckin' wit our family again. I hate them, Taurus. They took our baby and we couldn't do shit to protect her. What the fuck kind of parents do that make us? I'll tell you what kind. That make you a bitch of a parent, and me a triflin' ass mother. We both pussies, and not the good kind. I'm talkin' that infected yeasty shit that can't be cured."

She looked up into her rearview mirror. "And now these muthafuckas wanna get behind me. I ain't got time for this shit right now. Yo you got heat in here, right?"

"Ain't no question about it. It's a Tech .9 right under the seat," I said, leaning down and grabbing it. As soon as I did, the bitch ass police turned on their lights, signaling for us to be pulled over. "Baby, just be cool and pull over right there by that bus stop."

She smiled. "Today just ain't our day, is it, baby?"

I handed her the Tech and she put it right on her lap with her finger on the trigger. "Do you, boo. I feel like mafuckas just askin' for this shit this mornin'."

I looked into my passenger's side mirror and noted that it was only one officer in the car. He casually stepped out of his vehicle and made his way to the driver's side of the truck.

As soon as he got to the window, Princess rolled it down, and he stepped in front of it with his hand on his service weapon.

"Ma'am, I'm gon' need for you to keep your hands on the steering wheel, and tell your passenger to keep his on the dashboard where I can see 'em."

She laughed. "Baby, you heard him, right?"

I nodded, placing both of my hands on the dashboard before looking back over to him. "Is that cool, Mr. Officer, suh?" I asked, sounding like one of the characters from Roots.

The white man gave me an appreciative but cautious look. "That's right enough fine, thank you kindly." He turned his eyes back to Princess. "Ma'am the reason why I stopped you is because it looks like your left back tire may have a slow leak, you might wanna get that fixed." He touched the brim of his police hat and kinda nodded. "You two have a nice day and I think I'mma turn in myself. It's gettin' right around time fo my shift to end and I wanna drop this old vehicle off at the station and get on home. Looks to be an enjoyable day startin'."

Princess turned her head to the side. "You mean to tell me that you pulled me over so you could have this long ass conversation that don't nobody give a fuck about but you?" She frowned. "Then you talkin' about an enjoyable day. Don't you know that my daughter got kidnapped today? That I lost my mother-in-law to be, and my sister. And you runnin' around pullin' people over because you wanna be nice. Why wasn't y'all so nice when your comrades killed that unarmed black man last week? Or what about that sista that got beat to death in that police station right down the street there?" She pointed out of the window.

"Now you hold on just one fuckin' minute. All I was tryin' to be was nice to yo black ass and tell you that your fuckin' truck is losing air. I didn't ask for you to go all ghetto on me, sista girl from the hood." He did the sir quotes with his fingers. "That son of a bitch that got shot to death by one of my officers deserved to die. He was a low life drug dealer, and the world could do without him. And that black bitch should 've shut the fuck up when we told her to, but she was so high on dope that she didn't listen. Every time we gun down one of you dirty black motherfuckers it makes the job that much more fun. All of you niggers are supposed to be in prison, or somewhere dying from AIDS. It's gotten so bad that most of my white counterparts are takin' jobs on the force just so we can beat you niggers like we used to do on the cotton fields. And if we gotta put a bullet in yo black filthy flesh, well that just keeps things interestin'. I hate the smell of you niggers, and the only jewelry you look good in is handcuffs." He curled his upper lip. "Now I tried to be nice, but since you wanna force my hand, why don't you step out of the vehicle so I can pat search you and stick my fingers up your stretched banana twat." He grabbed the handle of the door and opened it.

Princess looked at me and smiled. "One of the best killings ever."

As soon as he grabbed her arm, she grabbed his head, stuck the Tech in his eye socket, and pulled the trigger. Blood splattered all over my face after the *bap-bap-bap-bap-bap* sounded. She pulled him in even further, slammed the Tech to the back of his head, and pulled the trigger, drenching us with his brains and tissue. It was like somebody had put a dynamite inside of his mouth and it exploded. The inside of my truck looked like it had been doused in red paint. It smelled like spoiled milk.

"That's what you get, you racist muthafucka. Now yo family can feel what theirs did," Princess said, pushing him off her lap.

I shielded my face after looking around, then I slid out of the truck, dropped low to the ground, and crept to the passenger side of his patrol car. I opened the door, got in, and closed it. The first thing I did was locate the dash camera. I broke it off, took the tiny CD out of it, and slid it into my pants pocket. Then I got behind the driver's wheel and drove along side of

Princess. I got out and opened the back door, and she helped me throw his ass into the back seat of the car. There was blood all over him, and his face was caved in with blood pouring out of it.

"What you finna do wit him, baby?" she asked looking overly excited. She got back into my truck and closed the door. There was blood all over her face, along with the scars that my father and brother had given her.

"I'm finna take his ass over to the old rail yard on Ashland and burn him up. It's a tunnel down there that I can drive this car into, and won't nobody look there for a few days. That should give us enough time to plan our next move. But fuckin' around wit a police officer will have the whole Memphis shut down."

"Well let's go then. I'mma follow you."

I stormed off in the car, and noted right away that it drove way smoother than my truck. Whenever I barely stepped on the accelerator, the car jerked forward, and started to pick up speed. I guessed that it was that Nitro fluid that they used in most stations. I could hear the dispatch on the radio reporting things from one squad car to the next. Before I had gotten into the police's whip, I noted that the car's number was B-60, so I was trying to see if I would hear that come up on the radio.

Princess drove close behind me. The sun had fully come up now. I knew that time was of the essence, especially since I recalled him saying that he was scheduled to get off work soon. I didn't know if he shared the squad car with another officer or not, but I didn't want to take any chances.

I pulled into the railway yard like fifteen minutes later with Princess trailing me. The rail yard was deserted for the most part, though it still had a few coaches that weren't attached to anything. There was about four of them spread out along the tracks. Once you crossed the tracks, passed a point, and made a left, there was a big tunnel that the old engineers used to fix the trains in. When my family first came to Memphis, me and Juice used to take lil' hoes there that skipped school. I wasn't fucking at that time, but he was, and I had witnessed him and his right-hand man down some broads in there. We also used to use it as a hide out when we ran from the police. I drove the cop car all the way into the tunnel, and parked the whip, before getting out.

Princess stepped out of my truck and came over to me. Standing on tippy toes, she kissed me on the lips and moaned into my mouth. "Damn, you drive me crazy."

I laughed, grabbed the keys out of the ignition, and used them to open the trunk of the car. I saw a flare gun, spare tire, a gas can, and a yellow box marked *military issued*. After sitting the gas can by my feet, I grabbed out the yellow box, knelt down, and opened it. Inside were four Kevlar armor piercing protective bullet proof vests. I smiled at that. We definitely were going to be in dire need of them down the line. "Baby, put this box in the back of my truck." I handed the box to her and watched her walk over and place it in the back of it.

Then I took the gas can and doused the policeman with gasoline. I poured it all down the split in his face and all over his clothes. I then took his uniform shirt off him, twisted it up, and stuck it in the gas tank. Then I took the AR-15 that was stuck against the glass in between the passenger and driver seat, and loaded that into the back of my truck, along with all the ammunition. After that, I set the car ablaze, and me and Princess drove out of the tunnel just as the car exploded in a loud *boom*.

Chapter 3

I was in the garage vacuuming and shampooing my truck down for the twentieth time, which I had been up all morning doing. I was trying to get every speck of blood and brain matter out of the interior or wherever it might have been hiding. I already had it in my mind that I was going to get rid of the truck that day anyway, I just hadn't figured out how.

"Baby, come in the house and chill for a minute," Princess said, walking up to me and rubbing my chest. "You been up for damn near two days. You gotta get some sleep or you gonna fall out." She had been in the house sleeping ever since we had made it home. I didn't know how she was able to shut her mind off like that, but I wasn't able to. I had so much going through my brain that I could barely think straight.

I looked over the truck one more time. "Alright, ma, it should be cool until we get rid of it later. I am tired as a mafucka, though," I said, wrapping my arm around her and leading her back into the house. I got to missing Jahliya as soon as I stepped into the living room from the garage because I saw her little pink jacket hanging on the back of one of the chairs at the table. I swallowed and felt butterflies come into my stomach.

"I'mma kill them niggas, Princess. Mark my words. I'mma kill them niggas in cold blood."

She nodded, leading me to the room. "It was her jacket for you too, huh?" She blinked and a tear fell from her eye. "As soon as I saw her jacket, I nearly had a nervous breakdown. I can't believe they took our baby. I pray that she's okay, your mother and Mary, too."

"Me too, ma." As soon as I got to our bedroom and hit the mattress, I was out like a light. I mean, I went into a deep sleep.

I didn't wake up until several hours later, and by that time, it was pitch dark outside. I would have stayed asleep, but Princess woke me up straddling me and pushing me in the chest.

"Look, Taurus, I just got some more bad ass news and before I break down, I need you to fuck the shit out of me until I cry. And I'm not playing either. Do you understand that?" she asked, unbuttoning one of my long shirts that she sometimes slept in, exposing her round succulent breasts, with areolas that damn covered the entire titty. Her nipples were already hard and standing out about an inch from her titties. She pulled on them to make them stretch even farther.

"I need you, daddy. I need you to heal me."

I sat up in the bed and rolled my head around on my shoulder. "I don't know what's the matter, but you already know I got you." I bucked my hips upward and flipped her off me, and then straddled her. I ripped the shirt all the way off her, taking the fat nipple of her left breast, sucking into my mouth, as I slid my hand into her panties.

"You need yo daddy to fuck you, baby, huh? You need me to take this shit from you like daddy s'pose to?" I said, sliding my two middle fingers deep into her hot wet pussy, making her arch her back, and open her legs wider.

"Yeah, daddy. Yo baby needs you. I need you to take me away from this pain like only you can. Please, daddy." She sat up and bit me on the neck.

I growled and pushed her back down to the bed, sucking on her neck roughly while my fingers ran in and out of her at full speed. Her little legs were spread wide. I could feel the satin material of the panties rubbing against the back of my hand.

"Rip them muthafuckas off, daddy. Please. Don't play wit yo baby like this," she moaned, and arched her back as my thumb rubbed against her clitoris. It was oozing juices, very slippery. I ripped the panties off her, causing her ass to rise from the bed a little bit. Once they were free, I pushed her knees to her chest and sucked her whole pussy into my mouth, taking time to suck on each individual lip before slurping up her clitoris and rolling my tongue all around it.

"Yes, daddy. Eat yo baby. Eat me good, daddy, please," she moaned, humping into my mouth and squeezing her own titties.

"Oh shit, daddy, I'm coming already. Your baby coming already, just keep nipping my clit wit yo teeth like that, please. Ahhhh. Ohhh. Shiiittt!" she screamed.

I had her juices all over my face, and I was loving the smell of her. There was nothing like the smell of some sexed pussy. That shit drove me crazy, and the taste had my dick harder than calculus. I sucked on her clit even harder, and slid three fingers into her while my tongue went 'round and round on her clit.

"Dadddeeee, yessss!" She started shaking and humping into my mouth at the same time.

As soon as she started to calm down, I got on my knees wit my dick out. I rubbed it around her wet lil' opening, and slid in until my balls slapped against her ass cheeks. Her pussy was tight and as hot as an oven on broil, as always.

"Give me this pussy, baby. Give daddy this shit," I plunged into her rough and deep, pushing her knees further into her chest, busting that pussy wide open. The headboard was beating against the wall like it was trying to go through it. The springs in the bed were squeaking so loud, it sounded as there were kids jumping on it.

"I can't take this shit, daddy. I can't take it. Uh shit! You fuckin' a hole in me. You too deep. Ah, my God. This shit so goooodddd!" she said right before screaming and shaking.

I felt her pussy walls vibrate, squeezing my dick like it was trying to strangle it. That good fluid got to building in my balls and I couldn't hold back no more. I wrapped my hand around her throat and squeezed, speeding up my thrusts.

"I'm finna come in you, baby. Daddy finna come, baby." I flipped onto my back and threw her with me, making her slam down onto my dick. I came all in her lil' pussy with her on top of me. All it took was three pounces, and I was coming deep in her womb while I held her ass apart, rolling my middle finger all over her asshole.

I laid her on her stomach while I kissed all over her ass and sucked on the back of her thighs. "Tell me what happened. What made you wake me up like you did?"

"We gotta take a trip to New Jersey," she said, spreading her legs wider making her pussy pop out.

I rubbed her swollen sex lips and kissed them, at the same time squeezing her booty, massaging it like dough. "Why is that, baby? What's out in Jersey?"

"My sister got a baby by this nigga that we all grew up wit. He been puttin' his hands on her again. This time, my aunt says he messed her up so bad that she's back in the hospital, in a coma. She said they found my sister in her apartment barely hangin' on to the edge of life."

I continued to rub her booty, trying to console her. "So what, we stop lookin' for our daughter to go out there and take care of this nigga or somethin'? I mean, what you thinkin'?"

She moaned as I planted delicate kisses down her sex lips and slurped up her running juices. "Nall, daddy, we still on bidness to track yo ol' man down. I just wanna shoot out there to Jersey and pay this nigga some street justice on behalf of my sister. I mean, if I don't hold her down, then who will?"

I licked up her thigh, then her pubic mound, and all the way up to her lips, until we were kissing and tonguing each other down. "You already know I'm down to do whatever for you. You my heart, and if ain't no other nigga gon' help you hold yo people down, you know this one right here is. After we get rid if this truck, we on the next flight."

In response, she had me get on my back, where she inhaled my dick, and sucked it until I couldn't get hard no more that night.

***

The next day, I sold my truck to my mans, Peto. He was a Brazilian kat that ran a chop shop. I went to high school with him, and we were always cordial. I knew from past experience, he would take the truck and chop it up right away, and that's exactly what we needed to happen. I didn't know if my truck was on fire or what, but I wasn't taking no chances.

Later that same night, me and Princess found ourselves on a plane, sitting in coach to try and blend in, on our way to Newark, New Jersey. When we got there, we rented a Buick Lacrosse through Enterprise.

"Baby, I think you gonna love my aunt. She super hood and she keep shit real at all times. I want us to stop by her crib before we go see my sister in the hospital. I just want you to hear everything that's goin' on from her mouth, and know that I love my sister wit all my heart. Okay, baby," she said, rubbing my chest and kissing me on the cheek.

"Like I said before, lil' mama, I'm gon' hold you down. However you need me to be there for you, I will be."

We pulled up to her aunt's duplex an hour later and I was surprised that she was waiting on the porch for us. As soon as Princess saw her, she jumped out of the car and they ran to each other and hugged, making all kinds of loud ass noises.

"I missed you, baby," her aunt said, hugging her tight.

"I don't know why you moved all the way down there wit Pac Man crazy ass. You know you my favorite niece."

Princess nodded. "I know, TT." She turned around and pointed at me. "TT, this is my baby daddy right here. His name is Taurus. I told you about him over the phone."

I walked over to shake her hand and she smacked it away. "Son, if you don't get yo ass over here and gimme a hug. We don't play that scary shit out east. We is a warm loving family. And since you got a baby with my niece, that makes you family, too." She hugged me tight and kissed me on the neck.

That caught me off guard. I frowned and took a step back, looking at her like her face was melting or something. "Did you just kiss me on my neck?" I asked wiping it away.

She closed her eyes. "I sho did. And the next time I get you to wrap them big ass arms around me, I'm gonna do it again, too." She grabbed one of my arms and squeezed my bicep. "Damn, now this a man right here, Princess, I know damn well that you don't be handlin' all of this."

She laughed. "I sure do. And I make sure he don't take it easy on me either." She looked up at me and sucked on her bottom lip, making herself look sexy as hell.

"I bet. Well before y'all go, you gonna have to let me test drive this whip, even if we have to do it together, so you can make sure I don't eat his ass alive. Damn, he fine! Y'all come on in this house."

"Taurus, don't mind her. I told you she was real as hell. That just mean she feelin' you, that's all, so don't be taken aback or nothin'," Princess said, pulling my hand so we could follow her aunt up the stairs.

As she walked in front of us, for the first time I could see that she was strapped. I mean, she had a big ass booty, and she was working that mafucka, too. I had to nod my head.

"Yo, on some real shit, if yo aunty really talkin' about playin' around wit us, I'm down. She got a fat ass booty and that lil' chubby thing workin' for her." I was serious as hell, too. Her aunt had to be about five-foot two, and about a hundred forty pounds. She was caramel skinned with shoulder length hair that made her look nice to me. I mean, all of that was cool, but I was jockin' the hell out of that fat ass booty. I wanted to rock that mafucka at least once.

Princess laughed. "Boy, you really think I'm 'bout to let you give my aunty some of my dick?" She raised her eyebrow.

I shrugged my shoulders. "Why not? We ain't gon' be comin' back out here no time soon, and she got a big ass booty. I bet that shit good."

Her Aunty turned around and smiled. "It sho is, and you best believe I know what I'm doin'. But you okay, Princess. I ain't gon' hook yo nigga on this shit. I'mma give him a pass wit his fine ass. I'd tried to be yo aunty and yo baby mama.

Word is bond." She opened her front door, letting me and Princess step in.

The crib looked welcoming. She had all white leather furniture with the plastic still on it. It smelled nice, as if an incense was burning. It was clean and tidy, and there was a big ass TV hanging on the wall that had ESPN on it.

"Princess, yo daddy'll be here ina lil' while, too. I told you he back stayin' wit me, right?"

"Yeah, I know," she said, lowering her head.

"Damn, girl, you seem depressed. What's all that about?" she asked, having us take a seat on the sofa. When we sat down it sounded like a bunch of people eating on dry cereal.

"Nall, I ain't depressed or nothin' like that. I just ain't got time for all that drama. The only reason we're here is because we wanna find out what happened with Rahkell."

"Okay, ouch!"

"Nall, I ain't sayin' it like that. You know I love you, TT, but Jersey just ain't what's poppin' for me no more. I went through too much bull crap here, especially with him and my mom."

"Girl, I know. Calm down because I'm iust playin' wit you. But just let him know how you feel when he gets here." She shrugged her shoulders. "I don't know, but let me tell you what happened with Rahkell and Aaron. First of all, you know he got that girl snortin' that shit again." She shook her head. "She been tootin' that heroin like ninety going north, that's why Jaylen and Josiah stay with me now."

"Really? Where are my nephews now?" Princess asked.

"Well, Josiah is at school, and Jaylen is at daycare. They were both driving me crazy. I had to get they ass out of this house early this mornin'." She sat down on the love seat across from us and crossed her big thighs. The small skirt that she had on basically disappeared, and I could see her lace red panties. "Now, let me tell you what happened. That half breed nigga went to Rahkell's salon and beat her senseless in front of all her customers because she didn't want to mess with him no more. He say her and Tristina on the down low, that he caught them in the act. Long story short, he beat her into a coma last Thursday, and she was in it for two days. She woke now though.

Princess shook her head. "Well, we about to go holler at her to see what's good. Then I think that fool Aaron gotta pay for his sins because I'm tired of people puttin' they hands on my lil' sister. I know we ain't always got along, but she's still my heart. That will never change. What hospital is she at, by the way?"

"Beth Israel. You know, over there off Lyons Avenue and Parkview Terrace." She uncrossed her legs, flashing me them pussy packed panties, and then crossed them again, licking her lips.

"Oh yea, I know where you talkin' about."

TT looked me in the eye. "So, you gon' leave him here with me while you and your sister have a private moment?"

Princess sucked her teeth loudly, "TT, you not finna fuck my baby daddy. That's not happenin'. Now, I'll think about lettin' you suck his dick or somethin' before we leave, but right now that's up in the air."

Her aunty scooted to the edge of the couch and opened her legs wide. She pointed to her panties. "But look how wet he got me without even touchin' me. I know he got some good dick. I can just tell by the way he carry his self. At least let me see what he workin' wit." She licked her lips, and sucked on her bottom lip, looking me right in the eye.

Princess turned toward me. "You wanna let her see yo dick so she can get off my case and we can get out of here?" She reached into my lap and squeezed it.

I laughed and stood up. "It is what it is." I unzipped my True Religion shorts and whipped out my shit, stroking him back and forth until he stood up with an attitude.

TT dropped to her knees and walked across the floor never taking her eyes off my dick. As soon as she got directly in front of me, she looked over to Princess. "Can I, niece? Please." She begged.

"Alright, but you can't use your hands though." She picked up my dick and fed it to her aunt.

As soon as it got into her mouth, she moaned and tightened her lips around my helmet. "Damn, his dick fat, and it taste good, too." She sounded like somebody trying to talk with their thumb in their mouth.

When she got to sucking me harder and harder, I couldn't do nothing, but grab Princess and tongue her little ass down. Her aunty had pulled her titties out, and I saw where she got the big nipples from. It must've run in their family. I fucked her hard in the mouth, and she let me do it until I carne down her throat.

"Now let me hold it, Princess, please. I gotta squeeze that nut out," she said with my dick resting against her cheek.

"Go ahead, but hurry up because we gotta get out of here."

She sounded irritated, and I could also see that she eyed the woman with annoyance.

TT acted like she didn't even exist once she put my dick in her hand. She squeezed it, and wrapped her fist around the bottom, squeezing it and pumping upward making my come squirt out of my pee hole. That shit felt good as hell, especially when she wrapped her mouth back around me and made me come again. It took all the will power that I had in me to not play with her pretty ass titties. She had popped them over the top of her bra, and both of her nipples were super hard. That shit looked enticing. She ended her play by rubbing my dick head all over her nipples.

The car ride was quiet for a minute as we drove to the hospital. I felt like there was something on Princess's mind.

"Yo, why you bein' so quiet, ma?"

She shrugged her shoulders. "I'm just thinkin' about my sister, that's all." She pulled into the parking lot of the hospital and parked. "I wanna kill that nigga. I never did like his punk ass." Her eyes got low, and her upper lip curled.

"Yo, who you talkin' about?" I asked, letting my seat back a little bit.

"My sister baby daddy, Aaron. I always hated him ever since they first got together. I wish he would have put his hands on her in the beginning. We could have nipped that shit in the bud then. But he waited until they had their second kid to start all this bullshit. Now, he got her fuckin' with that heroin again. Fuck, I hate that nigga!" She slammed her hand against the steering wheel.

I reached over and stroked her soft cheek. "Don't worry, we gon' body that nigga before we leave from up here. That's my word."

Chapter 4

"I ain't wanna start doin' that shit again. But he been puttin' me through so much, that it's all I can do to maintain my sanity. I be wakin' up suicidal every single day. I'm tired of goin' through all of this shit," Rahkell said before she broke into a fit of coughs.

Princess sat on the bed and rubbed her back, then put the straw to her lips so she could suck up the juice. "It's gonna be okay, Rahkell. I'm here for you now."

Princess and her sister looked just alike, but Rahkell had a bit more weight on her. She looked like she was dehydrated. Her hair was all over the place. I could see the visible wounds from her apparent abuse.

"How is my niece doin'?" Rahkell asked, trying her best to sit up. The bed squeaked, and she knocked over a cup that was on the tray in front of her.

Princess picked it up and kissed her on the cheek. "She's okay," she lied, looking me in the eyes. "She down in Memphis with her grandmother. We was gonna bring her out here, but decided against flyin' with her too soon."

Rahkell nodded. "That's what's up. Well, when you do get back to her, you make sure you kiss her for me and tell her that her aunty loves her. I think I wanna fly down there for Thanksgiving this year anyway. I mean, if that's okay with you guys?" She looked from Princess over to me.

"Yeah, babe, that's fine. But for now, you just get some rest so you can get up out of here." She helped her lay back. "I love you."

"I love you, too, Princess, and you make sure you come back before you leave, okay?"

"Yeah, we will." She kissed her again. "Hey, before I go, though, Aaron still lives over on Maplewood Ave, right?"

She nodded. "Yep, wit his dope fiend ass sister."

"Yeah, I thought so."

Princess didn't say a word to me when we got back in the whip, and since I ain't know what was on her mind, I decided to stay quiet until she pulled up in front of these grimy looking ass project buildings. As soon as we did, about ten dudes ran up to the car with dope in their hands, trying to push it through the windows that we had rolled down.

"Yo, son, I got that *piy-yow*. Take this shit and you'll be up all night, kid. Word is bond," said one dude wit dreads so long that they fell past his waist. He stuck his head in my window and I remember thinking that his breath smelled like pure shit.

I pushed his head back out. "Nall, nigga, we ain't lookin' for that shit." I mugged Princess as a nigga stuck his head through her window and held up about an ounce of Loud and another of dope that had a yellow tinge to it.

"Say, ma, this shit is sauce right here. Take this off my hands, and I promise you'll never regret it. This that A-1. Word to ya mother," said the skinny bald dude with glasses on his nose.

"Princess, what the fuck we doin' here right now?" I asked, ready to make her ass drive off. These niggas looked super gutta, like all they did was smoke dope and kill niggas all day. I wasn't hip to them east coast cats yet, but I knew from fucking with my best friend and right-hand man, Tywain, that they were grimy as fuck.

She held up one finger. "Yo, I need some heat, pa. Which one of you niggas wanna get rid of a burner for the low? I don't even give a fuck if it got a body on it."

The dread head nigga stuck his head back into my window. "Yo, what type you trying to locate, goddess. I got everything from handguns to assault rifles," he said with his breath funking up the car. It smelled like his tongue was taking a shit and forgot to courtesy flush more than once.

"I just need a few handguns, boss. You know, something like a .9, or a .45. I'll even fuck with some revolvers, long as you got the speed changers wit 'em," she said, pulling out a knot of money.

The dread head looked over his shoulder. "Yo, she got blue faces, son, and baby need them Star Wars." He stuck his head back into the car. "Yo, pull around to the back of the project and I'mma get you right. Don't mind them feens back there, either, just let them do them." He jogged away from the car and ran into the buildings.

Princess threw the car in drive and slowly pulled away from the curb. "Yo, I miss this hood shit. I grew up around here. I know these streets like the back of my hands."

I swallowed and looked at her like I had never seen her before. I couldn't believe how she was conducting herself. That shit was throwing me off, and turning me on at the same time. To me, it wasn't nothing like a hood chick that wasn't afraid to get knee deep into the streets. Shorty had hella heart and that shit was starting to make me feel some type of way about her even more. But even so, I had to make sure that she knew what she was doing. That was just that protector in me.

"Yo, we finna follow these niggas into a dark alley?" I asked, raising my eyebrow.

She shrugged her shoulders. "Yeah, why not? What you think finna happen in the middle of the street out here? We gotta duck into the back alley where it's good."

As she said that, she made a left, and then another right into an alley that had a light in the middle of it that blinked on and off. It gave the alley a very eerie feel. As soon as our car lights illuminated it, I saw a bunch of addicts walking around like they were Zombies. Some of them were laid against garbage cans with their mate laying on their chest. While others were sitting Indian style, shooting dope into their veins. Little ways away from them, there were others that rocked back and forth scratching themselves like something was crawling on them.

Princess pulled further down the alley, and they parted like lost cattle. A few times she had to blow the horn. "Get yo ass out the way, ma, before I hit you. I ain't got good eyesight like that. I'll run ya ass over and keep going." She laughed with her head out of the window.

"Calm down, Princess, and let's just handle business and get the fuck out of here," I said, looking around and feeling uneasy.

That alley looked like it was the place that fiends went to die. I even saw a few mafuckas laid out in the middle of the road, unmoving. Princess drove the car right over they ass and kept going. I ain't even ask her why. When we got to the middle of the alley, like fifteen niggas carne out of the gangway with helmets on that had lights on the ends. That shit looked crazy as hell to me. I ain't never saw no niggas strapped up like that. I started moving around uncomfortably in my seat, especially when they surrounded the car and all of them upped assault rifles and pointed them at the car.

Princess frowned. "What these niggas on?" she asked, trying to open her door, making the car's interior light come on.

I grabbed her arm. "Yo, what the fuck you doing? Sit yo lil' ass back."

The niggas mugged us for a long time not saying shit. Then we saw the dread head from earlier come through the crowd and walk over to Princess' window. "You can get out, lil' ma, I ain't gon' hurt you." He opened the door, and the interior light came back on, causing a dinging sound to go off.

She tried to get out but I held her arm. "You ain't goin' out there unless I'm wit you. These niggas about to kill both of us because ain't shit happenin'."

When she didn't get out right away, the dread head knelt down and looked into the car. "Yo, what's the biz, ma?"

"My daddy ain't tryna let me get out without him by my side. He feelin' like if you niggas on some fuck shit then y'all gon' have to kill both of us. That's just how it's goin' down. We ride to the dirt."

He started laughing and looked over at me. "So, you tellin' me that if I body her ass right here, you gon' die wit her? I mean, even if I say you can leave?" He curled up his upper lip.

"Whatever you do to her, you gon' have to do to me. This my heart right here."

He snickered. "Oh, you on some Captain Save a Ho shit, huh? Yo, Weezy, hand me that kay, boss."

I saw some lil' fat nigga with long dreads hand him an assault rifle. The fat nigga looked directly at me and laughed. "Yous a dead nigga now, kid," he said and stood behind the first dread head.

The first nigga took the kay and aimed it directly at Princess. "Yo, you know yo brother still owe me fifteen gees. I been waiting for you to get back in town so I could finalize this debt. I got word from up top to knock yo head off on sight, and that's just what I'm finna do." He cocked the assault rifle on the side and put it to her head.

I pulled her to me and grabbed the barrel of the gun. "Kill me, bitch ass nigga. Let her go!" I pulled Princess out of her seat and climbed over her. I took the barrel of the gun and put it on my forehead. "Pull the trigger. I'll be the debt. Pay me in full, nigga, but let her go."

He started laughing. "Yo, this nigga fa real, Princess. Thorough as a muthafucka!"

"I told you, cuz. That's why I'm down for my nigga. Now quit playing and let me get them bangers."

He stood up. "Yo, put that shit in the backseat of my lil' cousin whip. She good. I just wanted to make sure that she wasn't fucking wit some lame nigga from the south."

The back door opened and I could hear something heavy hitting the seat repeatedly, and then the door closed.

He knelt down. "By the way, my name Rex, homey, and Princess my lil' cousin. She my heart, too. I heard about what's cracking down there in Memphis and soon as she give the word, me and my brother Kevin gone shoot down there and regulate some shit, just giving you a heads up."

He stood back up and Princess climbed over me. "Yo, tell Kevin and Elise that I love them, and when I get situated I'm gone send for them to come and spend some time with my family. It's just right now that shit crazy but we gone get it together."

"I got you. Elise been asking about you anyway. You know she writing books and shit now. Ahmad Jr. big as hell, too. She completely bounced back after Ahmad got kilt. She love the shit out of Kevin, too, and he been holding her down. She put out these two books called My Brother's Baby mama, and them mafuckas doin' numbers. I'mma let her know that I hollered at you and that you gonna hit her up on Facebook."

"Alright, well you do that," Princess said, putting the car in drive.

He pounded on the top of the hood. "Y'all get out of here, and you take care of my cousin, Taurus. Me and the fellas gone be down there in Memphis soon. We gone touch down to cause hell. Trust me."

After we got back to her aunt's crib, as soon as I laid down in the guest bedroom that she let us stay in, I passed out. I had to be sleeping good as a muthafucka because when I woke up, I had slob all on the side of my face. It looked like somebody had poured water on the pillow I was sleeping on, and my mouth was dry as hell.

"Stop, daddy, get off me. I ain't on that shit right now." I could hear Princess saying in the distance. Her voice sounded close but funneled.

I rubbed the side of the bed next to me and saw that it was empty. That caused me to sit all the way up. I held my breath so I could hear what was going on better. It sounded like she was in the other room.

"Come on, baby girl. Don't tell me that you came all the way home and you ain't gone give daddy none of this body. I thought you loved me," he said, and then they were silent for a minute.

I started getting mad almost immediately. I didn't know who this nigga was, but I wasn't geeing for him being in the house while I was there. Then it sounded like she wasn't trying to fuck wit him on that level. I got to imagining some big ass nigga pushing up on my lil' baby and that shit made me jump out of the bed, and grab one of them pistols that we'd just bought from her cousin Rex. I lifted the bed and grabbed a .45, then slammed the clip in and cocked it back. I was ready to knock that nigga's head off on sight. If her aunt caught me then I'd just have to body her ass, too. Princess would understand, or else we'd just have to argue about that shit later.

"Daddy, I love you, but I don't wanna fuck you right now. Besides, I'm not no lil' girl no more. I don't need my daddy the way I used to when we were living together. I'm grown now."

"But, baby girl, who was there for you when yo mama put you out of the house and beat you down in the middle of the street? You remember that?"

"Yeah, daddy, I do, but things are different now."

"You remember how I used to hold you, rubbing on that lil' booty. And then when my baby girl got all emotional how I used to lay you back and eat that pussy until you was screaming at the top of your lungs. You remember how you used to be begging for your daddy back then?"

"Ummm, yes, daddy, but I can't."

I was getting heated by this point. I figured that they were in the room right next to me, so I slowly crept out of the room that I was in, and stepped into the hallway. That bedroom door was right next to the guest bedroom that we were sleeping in, and it was open enough that I could see what was going on inside.

Some muscle-bound nigga with a short greying afro had Princess up against the wall with his hands allover her ass. She had on a real short Victoria Secret's night gown from the Pink collection, and they were turned sideways to the door so I could see that his hands was all up her lil' gown. The gown was around her waist, and he had a handful of both ass cheeks with his fingers up her leg holes. I saw myself blowing this nigga's head off, and cutting it from his neck, keeping it with me at all times as a souvenir. I had never been more heated and jealous in my entire life. Every time she called him daddy, I wanted to snap the fuck out.

She tried to push his hands away. "Daddy, can you please stop? I'm not your little girl no more. I'm grown now. Can't you just accept that?" she whined.

"You always gone be my daddy's girl," he said, and sucked into her neck, pulling her panties down, and sliding his hand down the front of her crotch.

"Unnn shit, daddy. Please don't do that." She tried to grab his hand but he picked her up and slammed her on the bed. Throwing her legs apart and getting in between them. "I need some of my lil' girl. I ain't trying to hear that shit. Before you went to Memphis, it was my pussy, now you switchin' up the game. Can't nobody do you like me."

I was about to bust in the door when I felt a hand on my shoulder. I turned around, snatched TT into the air, carried her into the living room, and sat her down, putting my hand over her mouth.

Her eyes were bugged out of her head. I could feel her shaking in her lil' white beater and boy shorts.

"I'm about to take my hand away from yo mouth but I don't want you to make any noise. Just tell me who the fuck that is in the room right next to ours." I slowly took my hand away.

"That's my brother, Donnell. He Princess father," she said, looking like she was ready to shit herself.

I shook my head. "Nah, that can't be her real father. Is you talking blood related. Like he fucked her mama, and they had my woman together?"

She nodded. "Yeah, that's her real daddy. Why, what's the matter?"

I shook my head real hard as I felt my heartbeat speed all the way up. I ain't know what type of shit they had going on in the past, but I had an idea, and that didn't get to me. I had my own thing with my moms before, so I guessed every family had secrets. But what got me heated was that she wasn't trying to fuck with him on that level and he was forcing his self on her. I ain't fuck wit rapists on no level. To me, men that raped women and kids were supposed to be executed on sight, and if I could I would kill every last one that walked the face of the earth.

"TT, whatever you see me do, don't call the police. Just know that I ain't gone kill this nigga on the strength of you, and it being her father. But come on, I want you to see something, and then just fall back." I pushed her ahead of me until we were outside of the bedroom door. I opened it a little more for her to peer into it. "Look."

By that time, Donnell was between her legs and he had her gown around her waist altogether. He had her titties exposed, sucking all over them, and her panties were around her ankles. He looked like he was trying to put his dick in her because he was moving his hand crazy like in his crotch and his boxers were pulled down to his thighs. "Come on, baby girl. I can feel how wet this pussy is. Every time my head touch them lips, your juices stick to me. He wiggled his hips. "Ahhh shit, there we go." He closed his eyes and opened his mouth, moving his hips back and forth into her.

Princess moaned, and closed her eyes with tears falling down her cheeks. "Just hurry up, daddy, please. I don't want you to do this, but just hurry up."

TT looked like she wanted to bust into the room but I grabbed her and pulled her back into the hallway. "Be cool, ma', I got this. Just whatever you do, don't call the police."

She nodded with tears in her eyes. "Just don't kill him. But you make his ass pay." She punched her fist. "I knew he was fucking that lil' girl when she stayed here," she whispered. "Princess a do anything for her father's love after her mother gave up on her, and Donnell took advantage of that."

"Yeah, baby girl, damn this shit so good," he said, ramming into her at full speed now.

"Stop, please. Please, daddy, I'm begging you to stop."

"Fuck that, you my lil' girl. You-"

I busted through the door, running full speed. I picked his ass up and tackled him straight out of the window in the bedroom. Glass shattered all around us as we fell out of the window and into the backyard.

"What the fuck, man?" he said with blood all over his face. I pulled him up by his shirt and punched him right in the mouth, and then backhanded him like I was pimping his ass, on some Gorilla shit.

"Taurus, baby, please don't kill him," Princess yelled with her head sticking through the window. She started to climb out of it, but had to stop and break some more of the glass around the window pane.

"Yo, this man bidness. You stay yo ass over there. This nigga still think he daddy, but I'm yo muthafucking daddy now. You my baby girl, and that's the last of the pussy he'll ever get from you. You understand that Princess?"

"Yes, daddy. Yes, I do." She dropped to the ground in the backyard. By this time Donnell was standing up with his hands in the air like he ain't won't no trouble. "Yo, you can have her, lil' brother. That shit ain't that serious. I just wanted to fuck, that's all."

Princess was on her way over to break us up, but stopped in her tracks when she heard that. She blinked tears. "Yeah, that's all it was?" She swallowed and started bawling. "You know what, fuck him up, Taurus. Heal my past by getting all in his ass. You my daddy, now and forever."

That was all I needed to hear. I rushed him and hit him so many times in his face that I lost count. Then I scooped him and dumped him on his neck. He fell flat on his back and just laid there. I straddled him, and put the pistol in his mouth. "Bitch nigga, open wide."

He opened his mouth all the way and I tried to damn near make him swallow it. I heard him gagging on it, and that shit got me excited. I jammed it further down until he was choking on the barrel. With my other hand, I was holding down his forehead. "Please. Please, don't kill me," he said and sounded like he was talking with a mouthful of ice cubes.

I jammed it a little further down his throat until he threw up all over my hand and the pistol. That shit ain't phase me at all.

"Listen here, nigga, if you ever touch my baby girl again, or even call her yo baby girl, I'm gone cut small pieces from yo body until I kill you. Then I'm gone cook you, and I'm gone make my baby girl eat yo bitch ass, and we gone shit you out together. You understand that?"

He nodded with vomit all over his face.

"Now when I take this pistol out yo mouth, I need you to say two things. First, I need you to apologize to my baby girl for hurting her throughout her whole life, and then I want you to tell her that you ain't her daddy no more, I am."

And that's just what he did.

Chapter 5

"Baby, trust me now. When you just hoisted me up, I looked into the window and I saw his ass sitting up against the wall with a belt around his arm, sticking a Syringe into his veins. All you gotta do is wait until I open the back door, and then you come in on business." She paused, and then smiled wickedly. "You know what, fuck this. I wanna body his ass. I mean, Rahkell my sister, right?"

I nodded, and tightened my hand around the steering wheel. We were parked in the alley behind a dope spot that Aaron was staying in. Princess was ready to head back to Memphis to find our daughter, and I was too. But before we left, she wanted to body her sister's baby's father, and I was cool wit it.

"Yeah, she is your sister, but I wanna fuck something up too, though," I said, leaning over and kissing her on the cheek.

"Nall, I got this. All I need you to do is to go and knock on the door, and as soon as they open it, they gone invite you in and ask you what's your drug of choice. Once you get in, I want you to lay they ass down, and then I'mma come through and cause hell," she said, licking her thick lips.

I wanted to fuck my baby right there. Every time she got on some gangsta shit like I was accustomed to being on, that shit turned me on more than anything. "A'ight, we gon' rock how you sayin', but if anything look crazy, I'm killin' mafuckas. I gotta protect my Princess."

She smiled all sexy like. "Aw, so you embracin' yo daddy roll to the fullest, huh?"

I grabbed her head and we started sucking all over each other's lips, making all kinds of loud freaky ass sounds that had my dick harder than a gang banger.

After our lust session, I stepped on the porch and knocked twice on the door before somebody started to open it. There stood short white lady with crust all on the side of her face. She had cold all in her eye, and her hair looked wilder than a monkey in the jungle. "Can I help you?" she said with her breath smelling like her tongue was passing gas. That shit went right up my nose, and damn near made me throw up.

I started scratching my arms, and rubbing my shoulders. "Look, I need a place I can do my shit at. I'll share a gram with the house owner, but that's all because I'm trying to zone, baby." I closed my eyes and jerked a lil' bit to really play my role.

She scratched her head and looked over her shoulder. "Well, honey, you can come on in. It ain't but me and my brother, and he got his own stuff right now, so you'd just be sharin' wit me, and I ain't greedy." She licked her crusty lips.

I walked past her into the house. "I know you ain't, and even if you was, you ain't gon' be greedy wit me."

As soon as I stepped into the door, this god-awful smell hit me in the face so hard I wanted to throw up my guards to fight it back. I mean, it was putrid. It smelled like ass and sugar. I pinched my nose. "What the fuck is that smell?" I looked around and saw Aaron still sitting up against the wall in his drawers.

The house didn't have no furniture in it at all. I mean, it was empty like they just moved in. There were beer cans all over the floor. Roaches crawled over the carpet in groups of fives. They were so big that they looked like frogs, damn near.

They had the nerve to have a Pit Bull that was so skinny he looked like a Weiner dog.

"Aw, baby, what you smellin' is the groove. The longer you go without washin' yo ass, the longer the dope stay in yo system. That's heroin 101, baby." She walked pass me and into the living room.

I hurried and unlocked the door back for Princess, then followed her in. I watched her sit down Indian style with her funky legs open. She ain't have no panties on. Her blonde bush looked yellow and smelled like spoiled fish. I could see yellow shit oozing out of her labia, and that made me damn near throw up.

Aaron slapped his self on the cheek, and nodded out.

"So, go ahead, honey. Pull out the good stuff and let's party hearty." She rubbed her stanky ass pussy. "Then you can fuck my twat with that big dick I know you packing. I can tell cause you got real big hands."

I know Princess was wanting this lick to be all hers, but if I didn't get shit jumped off, I was gone contaminate the crime scene by throwing up everywhere. It was taking every bit of will power that I had to not vomit right in that white bitch's face.

I held up one finger to her and knelt down in front of Aaron.

"So you Aaron, huh?"

He looked up at me with glossy eyes. "Yeah, man, and just who might you be?"

I was ready to blow his head off, him and the white bitch, and get out of there. I was probably gone kill the dog too, but then decided against it because he could eat on their flesh for a few days. You know, get some pay back for the way they starved him and shit. But as soon as I got ready to pull my pistol out, Princess came through the front door and locked it behind her.

The white bitch stood up. “Hey, Princess, how are you?”

Before she could even finish what she was about to say, Princess swung the pistol by the barrel and slammed the handle into her forehead. *Woom*! Blood started to spurt from the hole in her head immediately. “Shut up, bitch. I always hated yo hype ass.” As the white bitch fell to the floor, Princess got on top of her and started to beat her senseless with the handle of the gun.

Woom! Woom! Woom!

“You punk bitch, you allowed him to beat my nephews and hurt my sister. Now you payin’ for it.”

Aaron got up to try and run, but I hit his ass so hard that he fell up against the wall and slid down it in slow motion.

“Fuck nigga, you ain’t going nowhere. She got some shit planned for you.”

I watched Princess beat the white girl to a bloody pulp. Now, every time she brought the gun down into her face, it was only splashing up blood and brain matter.

“Baby, that bitch dead. Come on and kill this nigga now so I can enjoy this shit.” I got to feeling myself getting all giddy. I really wanted to see what she was going to do to this dude.

She stood up, looking down at the dead white girl. It looked like her head had been smashed in with a sledge hammer. It was mostly just mush now, like a smashed pumpkin. There was so much blood that the dog was licking it up.

Aaron shit on his self. I could smell it clear as day.

"Princess, I can explain what happened between me and Rahkell? You know she has a bad temper. I tried my best to-"

Boom.

I kicked him so hard in the chest that he flew through the wall that he was sitting against. "Yo, I hate when mafuckas try and cop pleas after they done fucked up. It's too late my nigga. Yo number already been called, and it's my Princess that's gone burn yo ticket." I picked him up and slammed him to the ground.

"Yo, daddy, pick his bitch ass up," she said, coming out of the small of her back with a big ass hunting knife. That mafucka looked like it was used to hunt Dinosaurs, it was so big and ridged.

I picked him up and put him in a full Nelson. "Please, Princess. I always been real respectful to you. I ain't never said nothing bad about you."

She walked up on him, grabbed his cheek, and cut it off. Then she threw it on the floor by his foot.

I opened my eyes so big that the skin of my forehead moved backwards. I had never seen no shit like that happen in front of me.

"Ahhhh," he hollered, before I put my hand over his mouth. His blood poured on to my arm and ran down the front of my shirt.

"That was for one of my nephews." She came forward and cut off his other cheek and threw it along side of the first one.

He started hollering even louder. I could feel his hot breath on my hand. I don't know why but I just busted up laughing like a muthafucka. Dude was screaming like a bitch, and it was funny to me. I hated niggas that put they hands on females, so I felt like he was getting what he deserved.

"That's for my other nephew. And this is for me." She pulled his nose and sawed it off real slowly, and if I thought he was screaming before, I hadn't heard anything yet. As she was sawing it off, his blood kept on spurting into the air.

"I never did like you, Aaron. You a mafuckin' pervert. You don't think I remember catchin' you sniffin' up my dirty panties when you got them out of the hamper. Nasty mutha-fucka." She cut his ear off and threw it in a pile with the rest of his parts. Then she did the same with the other ear. By that time, I had so much blood all over my hands that my grip was slipping as he wiggled around in front of me.

"Boo, kill this nigga because he wigglin' around too much."

She nodded, "Okay."

She stabbed the knife right into his crotch and pulled it upward, slicing a big split in his torso. All of his insides started to pour out of him. It sounded like somebody had threw a bucket of water on to the concrete. It smelled like hot plastic. She looked down on him as he shook, slowly dying in a pool of his own mess.

"Fuck nigga, that's what you get."

I pulled her into my arms, and kissed her on the forehead. "Yo, fuck this nigga, let's go get something to eat after we get cleaned up."

***

"Mama, let me see our daughter again," I said, looking into my phone. We had just found out that our plane would be leaving in the next half hour after it had been delayed for six. It was snowing like crazy outside. It looked like we were stuck on an all-white sheet of paper. We sat in the lobby waiting to board our flight.

"Hold on, son."

The next thing I saw was Jahliya's little face come into the screen. I felt tears rolling down my cheeks almost immediately. She had her little eyes closed, but as she breathed in, dimples came across her cheeks, Dimples that she had received from me.

"Can you see her?" my mother asked, trying to position her phone the right way.

"Yeah, I see her," I said with my voice breaking up.

"Look, Princess."

She got up and took my phone away from me. Peering into the screen. Then she started crying. "I want my baby, Taurus. Ain't no good reason for this dude to have our child. This some bull crap and you know it."

I wiped my tears away. "Yeah, boo, I know."

"How has she been, mama?" Princess asked, sitting on my lap. She wrapped one of her arms around my neck. I could smell her powder fresh deodorant mixed with a lil' sweat, and I liked it. I liked all her natural scents for some reason.

My mother's face appeared back on the screen. "She doin' good, baby. She's eatin' okay, and I keep her away from all of the drama."

I shook my head. "Yo, where are y'all stayin' right now?"

She looked like she was about to answer but then the phone was snatched out of her hands by my father. He looked into the screen and frowned. "This visit is now being terminated. You want your daughter back? First, you gotta survive Juice's army. If you still are alive in two weeks, then I'll send you your child by Deborah," he said, speaking in terms of my mother. Then the phone went dead.

"Yo, so why you ain't tell me that you was fucking yo old man?" I asked Princess as we flew over the states one after the other. She was laying her head on my shoulder, and I kinda whispered it into her ear even though there was nobody sitting next to us.

She sat up, gave me a crazy look, and shrugged her shoulders. "I didn't have no reason to bring that up. Just like you ain't tell me about you and your mother."

I held up my hand. "Yo, wit my mother was different. You see how dude be treating her. She ain't never felt love from a man before. And dude ain't touched her in years. My mother was broken, and lost. I did nothin', but heal her because she needed me."

Princess shook her head. "Nall, I get that, which is why I never said nothin' about it when KO brought it up in the house." She exhaled. "I just don't want you to start judgin' me and shit. I think you love me somewhat right now, and if we get to delving into my past, then your opinion of me might change, and I can't handle that because, just like your mother ain't never had a man love her for real until you, neither have I."

I kissed her on the cheek. "I'll never stop bein' crazy about you. Remember, I'm daddy now, and you my baby girl. I'm gon' always protect you, and love you harder than anybody in this world. Never forget that."

She nodded and took a deep breath, then exhaled. "My mother was abusive as hell. She used to beat me all the time, when I was little, so bad that my baby sister, Rahkell, used to have to step in to get her off of me. I think she beat me so bad for every little thing because she hated Donnell so much. Anyway, when I was sixteen, I got caught givin' my boyfriend head in the stairwell at school. He wanted to fuck but I wasn't ready for all of that, mentally nor physically, so I got to watchin' pornos and got practicin' on a lollipop, tryin' to get my head game up to par. Long story short, I really liked the boy that I had been dealin' wit at the time, but instead of lettin' him fuck, I gave him some head, and got caught doin' it because this guy busted out the window in the hallway that led to the stairwell. The principal played back the entire footage, and there I was ten minutes earlier doin' that with him. When my mother got me home after findin' out, she beat me so bad that I wound up in the hospital for three days. After I was released, she kicked me out the house and I moved in with my father. He ain't waste no time goin' in on me. He coddled me at first. You know, bein' all nice and shit, buyin' me stuff, and tellin' me how beautiful I was, and how special I was to him. You know, just makin' me feel good, and tellin' me things that no other person ever had before. My mother never gave me compliments, and I went above and beyond to please her. I mean, anything that you could think of, I did it for her. Yet she was cold as ice toward me my whole life, with the exception of my sweet sixteen birthday party that she spent damn near two gees on. But I can't even tell you that I enjoyed that day because she beat the shit out of me the same day. My father treated me like a princess, until one day, he simply snatched me up, pulled my pants down, and pushed my knees to my chest. He ate me out before doin' the most to me. I mean, I felt some type of way about it in the beginnin', but at that time, he was the only one givin' me love and affection." She took a deep breath and exhaled.

"I had like four good friends back in the day, around that time, and three out of the four of them had weird shit goin' on at home, similar to my situation. If it wasn't their ol' man, it was their brother, or *brothers*. And they made it seem like it was the most natural thing in the world. And I guess over time, I started to convince myself of the same thing. But every time he put his dick inside of me, I wanted to kill him. I despised the fact that his definition of a lovin' father, was to have his daughter sexually. I think that's why it's so easy for me to kill men. But I hate most women, too, and I think that comes from detestin' my mother subconsciously." She turned to look at me head on. "So, do you still love me or what?"

I hugged her and kissed her juicy ass lips. "Most definitely, and even more so now because we both had skeletons in our closet that we released to each other."

She nodded. "But I still wanna know how it all started with you and your mother, though. I mean, you always hear about that father daughter shit, but a person would never think that a mother would turn to her son, even though I'm pretty sure it happens behind closed doors a lot."

"Just like you kept shit one hunnit wit me, I'm gon' do the same wit you."

"I'd expect no less."

The plane jerked real hard, and the lights went out and then came back on. There were a few screams off in the distance. I opened my window to look out of it and saw that it was storming with lightning shooting across the sky. I found that crazy since before we got on the plane, it was damn near a blizzard outside.

"Attention, passengers, we need everyone to stay in their seats and to fasten your seatbelts. We're experiencing a little turbulence, and it should be a little rocky for the next five minutes until we exit the storm. Thank you for your cooperation."

We made sure our seatbelts were clicked and I wrapped my arm around her, and kissed her forehead. "If this mafucka go down-"

"Then we die together," she said, finishing my sentence.

I smiled. "Anyway, on some real shit, I always had this crazy crush on my moms that was innocent. I hated the fact that I had the father that I did, and that she was married to him. It's fucked up because I can't ever remember a time where my mother was happy or dude did somethin' special for her. All I can remember is him beatin' her, and making her cry. Anyway, I always wanted to be the one to heal her. To save her and take her away from him. Nothin' breaks down a little boy more than seeing his mother bein' abused and he can't do nothin' about it. I'd always be the one that cleansed her wounds after the damage had been done. But deep down, I had always wanted to be the one to prevent it. Yo, long story short, when that nigga got knocked this time, we just sorta started comin' at each other. My mother always been fine to me. The coldest female I had ever seen in my life. I was cursed with that Oedipus complex from birth. So, when shit got hot and heavy at my aunt's crib out in Jackson, I just rolled wit it. I don't regret that night. That was my first time ever seein' her really happy and satisfied. And if I had to, I would do it again because it made me feel like I was healin' her." I looked off into the distance, remembering that night. Then I smiled.

"So, it only happened one time?"

I nodded. "Yep."

Princess sucked her teeth loudly. “Man, y’all ain’t do shit. I’m thinkin’ you been makin’ love to her for years. It only happened one time, boy bye.”

I started laughing, and held her tighter.

Chapter 6

"Taurus, who is this bitch on the phone, asking me to talk to you all rude and shit?" Princess asked, bringing my phone into the bathroom while I was showering. It felt good to have the hot water beating off of my skin.

"Yo, what the name say on it?" I asked sticking my head out of the curtain.

"It say Blaze. Is this Tywain cousin from out in Houston that you was speaking about before. Didn't I meet her?" she asked, looking at the phone like it had disrespected her.

I stepped out of the shower, dried myself off as best as I could, and grabbed the phone. "Yo, this business right here. Calm down, lil' mama."

She pursed her lips. "Omm huh. Yeah, I bet. Well you better tell her that next time she call to be a little more respectful. Let her know it's a new sheriff in town." She walked out of the bathroom with her boy shorts all in her ass. It looked so damn good.

As soon as I started Face Timing wit Blaze, I could see that she was laughing. "Damn, sista girl standing on yo ass. I ain't expect no turn of events like this." She started giggling.

I had met Blaze for first time when my father went to have a business meeting with this famous birdman by the name of Jerry Walker. She was my right-hand man's cousin, and she was fine as a muthafucka and real freaky in that sack. She was a real famous stripper with a body so cold that every club she went to she was headliner status. Her name rang bells in the exotic dancing world. She was trying to put me on some real money out in Clover City, where she stayed down on Houston. She had a lot of underworld political connects that she knew could make me a rich man. In exchange for everything, all she wanted was my pipe, and for me to treat her every time I fucked her brains out. She was what you would call dick-whipped.

"Yeah, that's my baby girl right there. You know how shit goes. But what's good?"

"What's good is that I'm laid up at the Hilton and I'm trying to have you fuck me into a coma. I'm also ready to put you in the game with my cousins Flip and Screw. They run the whole Clover City and wanna fuck wit you on that level if you're still down to get some real money."

Ten minutes later, I was arguing with Princess as she sat on the edge of the bed in our hotel room. "Yo, so you finna go all the way over there to fuck this bitch just so she can put you in wit some niggas that we don't even know? What about our daughter? When we finna get to tracking her down? And plus, you already got plenty shit going on in Memphis that you ain't attended to yet. Martell them been blowing me up like crazy. What's good wit that?"

I kept getting dressed. I had to see what this bitch was talking about. I knew that once we finished tearing Memphis up, we was gone need a new location. I felt like Houston would have been perfect. "Yo, like I told you, this shit been in the works. I gotta meet wit her, and then we gonna find my punk ass father and Juice, and body both of them niggas in cold blood."

"I guess. I just don't like the thought of you fucking some other bitch while I ain't there. It's one thing if I'm present but it's a whole other when I'm not. I feel jealous as a muthafucka. I damn near wanna shoot you in both yo knee caps just to prevent you from going."

I laughed. "It ain't gotta come to that." I knelt down in front of her. "You know you my baby, so why you bugging? We ain't never talked about being on some one on one shit anyway, right?"

She stood up and pushed me out of her face. Then she walked into the bathroom and slammed the door. "I ain't think I had to spell the shit out for you. It should've been implied. Now you talkin' about going to fuck off wit some other bitch."

Boom! Boom!

It sounded like she was punching the wall or something. I walked to the door and jiggled the handle until it opened. She was sitting on the edge of the tub, holding her left hand. I knelt down in front of her and grabbed it. "What the fuck you just do?"

She yanked it away from me. "Taurus, just go handle yo biz, man, so you can get yo ass back here."

***

I met up with Blaze about fifteen minutes later. She was parked outside of a Burger King past the lights in Glenview.

As soon as I got out of my new STS rental, she opened the door to her Audi A6, and ran to me crossing the parking lot. She ain't stop until she jumped in my arms and wrapped her legs around me. I caught her in the air, and she started sucking on my neck right away. I ain't gone even lie, when she first did that shit, even though it felt kinda good, I got to feeling guilty as hell, like I was violating Princess. I mean, we had never talked about being exclusive or nothing like that, but after knowing her history, and releasing myself into her, I just felt like we were connected in a way that was indescribable. And that was fucking wit me a lil' bit, especially since I had a thing for Blaze. I just had to remember that I was on business, and the play wit her was strictly that.

As she wrapped her legs around me, I held her in the air by her thick ass cheeks, which were encased in some tight ass Donna Karens. She smelled good, as always, and that was another reason why I had a thing for her. "Baby how you been?" I asked, trying to sit her back on the ground, but she wasn't going. She kept her thick legs wrapped around me wit her face in the crux of my neck.

"I missed you so much. You all I been thinking about. It's like ever since I met you I been messed up in the head, and even though I'm out here getting money, it don't feel right because I'm not spending it on you." She licked my neck and then got down.

We ended up at her hotel room, where she popped the cork on a bottle of Raspberry Champagne, and let the fizz pour over her fingers. She had already changed into a real short Victoria Secret negligee, which was purple, and see through. As I laid back on the bed, eyeing her from her head to her perfectly painted toes, my conscience started getting the best of me. She turned around in a slow circle, letting me admire that body. When I saw how far that ass was poked out, my conscience started going away. I got to remembering how good her juice box was, and that made my dick rise, and lay up against my stomach.

"What's the matter, Taurus? What, you don't like what you see no more?" She turned around and wiggled her thighs, making her ass jiggle. Then she spread her legs and bent all the way over, and I saw how her tight panties went all up her ass, and cuffed her fat ass pussy. When I saw her lips down there, I was ready to wreck some shit.

"What?" I got up and grabbed her by her hair roughly. "Who you think you playin' wit? Huh?"

She gasped. "What are you talkin' about?"

"Shut up." I yanked on her hair, exposing her neck, bit into it, and then sucked on it before picking her ass up and crashing into the wall with her. I was cupping that big ass. I yanked them panties to the side and slid my three fingers in between us, and worked them into her with blazing speed.

"Ahhh, shit, here you go. Here you fuckin' go, Taurus, already, baby," she moaned with her mouth wide open. Her pussy juices dripped all over my hand, off of my wrist, down my forearm.

I tongued her ass down, then walked over and threw her on the bed on her stomach. I pushed her face into the mattress, and kicked her legs apart like I was about to search her. "I'm about to wear this ass out, then you gon' buy me a new truck because I don't feel like spendin' my own money. You got that shit?"

"Yes, baby. Whatever you say, just beat my pussy in. Knock my shit out of alignment like you always do. Please." She pulled her ass cheeks apart and sucked on her bottom lip in total submission.

I slid the rubber onto my dick and popped my thumb into her ass, at the same time driving into her so hard that I fell on top of her for a brief second. When I got it together, I started fucking her like I hated her. I mean, my dick was running in and out of that pussy at full speed, beating them walls loose, pulling on her hair, and smacking that big ole ass.

"Ahh shit, baby, you killin' me. You fuckin' me up right now, and I love this shit. Fuck, I love this shit. Please don't stop. I'll do anything just to make you keep goin'," she said, sounding like she was running out of breath.

I sped up the pace. "You say you'll do anything for me, right?" Her pussy walls got to gripping my dick and spitting hot juices all over it. I tightened my abs and stabbed into her.

"Yes. Yes. Anything. Ahhhh shit, I'm commminn'," she screamed and started shaking like she was having a seizure.

I got to running my thumb back and forth across her clitoris, smashing it and pinching it a lil' bit, until she started shaking so hard that I had to drive all the way into her and just leave my dick there while her walls percolated. Then I picked her up, slammed her on her back, and pushed her knees to her chest, busting that pussy wide the fuck open. I took full advantage, slamming into her juice box with all of my might and hitting the bottom while she screamed like I was killing her.

Afterwards, she sucked her own juices off my rubber, took it off, and sucked me while she told me how much she loved me. "Taurus, I'll to anything for you. I swear to God I will. Don't nobody fuck me like you do. You be treating my ass just like I need to be treated. I love you, I swear I do." She popped me back in her mouth and all I could think about was Princess.

"My cousins Flip and Screw want you to fly out to Houston this weekend so they can have a sit-down wit you. I guess your name ringing back in Clover City. They know about you and how you and Tywain handled business with Orange Mound and Black Haven. They say they want that same product, and got it through the grapevine that you fuck wit that nigga Hood Rich out of Chicago. Is that true?"

I shrugged my shoulders. "Somethin' like that."

"Well anyway, they been talking about that heroin that you got connects to. You know, that Rebirth stuff that make them feens feel like they gettin' high for the first time every time. They say if y'all can have a sit down on that topic, then you can discuss the eight apartment buildings I wanna give you in Clover City. They promise you protection and guidance in the new land. They already know that Tywain is yo right hand man. That's family, so it's good."

She rubbed my dick all over her face and kissed the head. I think she had some sort of fascination with big dicks because most of the times when we got together, all she wanted to do was play with mine.

"Yo, I'm tryna come out there as soon as possible, so see if you can arrange a sit down in a few weeks or so."

She smiled. "I just wanna make sure you out here eating, baby. That's the only thing that matter to me." She popped me back into her mouth and started sucking like a porn star that was running out of time. Then she climbed up my body and put my dick back into her, before riding me with her head back and face to the ceiling. "Aww shit, aww shit, aww, aww, yes, daddy, shit yes. Give me this dick. I love it. I love it, baby." She bounced up and down on me and squeezed my chest. Running her hands all over my abs. Before it was all said and done, I would fuck her on the balcony with her hanging halfway off of it.

When I got back to my hotel room, I damn near snapped. As soon as I opened the door, there was Princess laying back on the bed with her legs wide open, and some pretty boy Spanish muhfucka between her thighs, eating her pussy like it was sushi. I mean, he had her legs cocked all the way open.

"Unn Unn, yeah, Roberto, eat me, baby. Eat yo mami."

I ran over and pulled this nigga up by his long ass curly hair, before dragging him across the floor. Princess crawled into the bed, and laid back on her arms, smiling at me. "I'll see you later, Roberto."

I was about to body this cat when I figured what she was doing. So instead, I just threw him out into the hallway with his clothes. "Yo, don't come back around her no more or its gonna be ugly for you." I slammed the door in his face, even though he ain't utter a word.

Princess got out the bed ass naked, walked up to me, and kissed me on the lips. "So how has your night been so far? I take it your meetin' went over well," she snickered.

I moved her out of my way, stepped into the bathroom, and turned on the shower, taking off my clothes.

She carne in and pushed me enough to make me stumble a little bit. "Yo, so you can go out and fuck another bitch, but when I do me, you give me the silent treatment. What type of fuck shit is that?"

"I ain't said shit about what you just did, Princess. I think that shit was a little childish, some high school type shit. But as long as you feel better, then it's good. I just feel stupid because, even while I was smashin' shorty, I was thinking about yo ass."

She crossed her arms in front of her. "Well ain't that some shit. At least you stopped to think about me before you fucked the bitch. Don't I feel special?" She rolled her eyes, and bumped me out of the way.

I grabbed her arm. "Yo, I don't know who you think you bumpin' out the way 'n shit, but this ain't that shorty."

She looked down at the arm that I had a hold of. "So, what you sayin'?" She jerked her arm away.

I grabbed it again. "I'm sayin' I'll spank yo lil' ass. Like I told you before, you my Princess now. So, I don't know how you use to dealin' wit other niggas, but I'll put some fire to that ass. Word is bond."

She looked at me for a long time and then squinted her eyes. "If you don't let my arm go we about to fuck this hotel room up. And my word is bond."

I tightened my grip. "Now what shorty?"

She reached up and smacked me across the face so fast that I didn't have time to duck. Then she stomped on my foot, and jumped on me, wrapping her legs around me and smacking me in the face again and again.

That shit got to hurting right away. I carried her back into the bedroom and threw her across the room. She landed on the edge of the bed on the opposite side. She gathered herself and then ran across the bed at full speed with anger in her eyes.

As soon as she jumped to land on me again, I caught her ass in the air and slammed her on the bed. "You wanna play these muhfuckin' games, right?" I trapped her, then sat on the bed with her stomach in my lap. I put my left leg over both of hers so that her ass was up in the air. "I'm finna wear this lil' ass out. I keep tellin' you who daddy is." I raised my hand and brought it down hard on her bare ass cheeks.

"Nooo, daddy!" She tried to wiggle out of my grasp.

Smack. Smack. Smack. Her ass cheeks vibrated and shook. I rubbed them for a second, and then *smack. Smack. Smack.*

She started kicking her legs once again. Every time she did, she would expose her sex, all wet and puffed up. I slid my hand between her lips, and played in her box while she moaned and bit into my stomach.

"Daddy, I'm sorry. Please don't hurt your baby no more. I'm gonna be good. I promise."

I picked her up and carried her to the shower that was still going, washing her body from head to toe, before crouching down and eating her juicy pussy while she lifted one of her legs over my shoulder. Then I scooped her up and fucked her against the shower wall while she sucked on my neck.

"You the best daddy ever, Taurus." Her voice broke up. "Just don't hurt my heart, please, because I need you daddy." Tears rolled down her pretty brown cheeks.

Chapter 7

"Taurus, I need for you to come and get me, your sister, and the baby, right now," my mother said, hollering into the phone so loud that it caused my ear to ache.

I sat up in bed, my dick falling out of Princess. Every time we slept in the bed together, we'd spoon and I would slide deep in her and fall asleep. When she felt me pull my piece out of her she, woke up.

"Daddy, what's the matter?"

I sat all the way up and turned on the lamp that was on the side of the bed. I held up one finger. "Mama, go ahead and tell me what happened."

"I just killed your father. I couldn't take that shit no more. Now I need you to come and get us because I don't know what to do."

Me and Princess got there an hour later. My father had moved them to some cabin deep in the woods, and right behind a swamp. When we got there, I slammed the door to the car and ran to the shack, beating on the door. It looked like it was built around the slave times. It was nothing but a little shack that had some bogus ass aluminum acting as a roof. One room, and I guessed they didn't even have no electricity.

When my mother opened the door, she had tears rolling down her cheeks and a black eye. She ran to me and wrapped her arms around my neck. "Baby, I'm so sorry. I just couldn't take it anymore. Please don't be mad at me."

I could feel her shivering against me. I held her tighter and kissed her on the cheek. "It's okay, mama. Where is he at?" I asked, leading her into the house.

Princess ran past us, into the house. "Where is Jahliya? Where is my baby?"

Mary came from the back of the shack holding her. "She's right here, sis." She bounced Jahliya up and down slowly, walking over to Princess' outstretched arms, and handed the baby to her.

"Come here, baby. I missed you so much," she cooed wrapping Jahliya in her arms.

I walked past and kissed her on the forehead as my mother led me to the back of the shack, where the bathroom was located. Right in the middle of the floor of the bathroom was my father. He had an ax sticking out the back of his head and a pool of blood around him. He still had his glasses on, eyes wide open. I could tell that she caught him off guard, probably pissing.

"Mama, what happened?"

"He raped your sister last night, and that was the last straw. Come to find out, it wasn't the first time."

I felt like I wanted to throw up. "What do you mean?" I asked dumbly, knowing damn well what she meant. I was just taken aback. I mean, I knew my father was a sick man, but I didn't figure that he'd actually stoop that low.

She came to me and put her head on my chest. "Yep, he been raping my baby since she was seven years old, and I never knew nothin' about it. She say he didn't go all the way wit her until she was thirteen." She broke down crying. "How could I have not known this stuff, Taurus? Am I that naive?"

I rubbed her back. "Don't even worry about it. Look, I gotta get y'all out of Memphis before Juice get wind of this. When was the last time he was here?"

"He left this mornin' at like three. He said he'd be comin' back sometime this afternoon."

"Alright, let's go."

When we got back to the front of the shack, for the first time, I noticed that there was nothing in there, other than one king sized bed. Other than that, the place was empty.

As soon as we loaded up into the car, I looked down the road and saw about four Jeeps headed our way. The path to the shack was a one way in and one way out path. he road that the Jeeps were traveling to come to us was also the road that we needed to exit on.

"Mommy, that's Juice 'nem right there, what are we gonna do?" Mary said from the backseat.

"I don't know, baby, you gotta ask your brother."

"What are we gone do, Taurus?"

Princess handed Jahliya back to my mother and came from under her seat with a Tech .9. "Yo, I'm about to start bussin' so cover my baby's ears." She cocked the Tech and rolled down her window.

I reached under my seat and grabbed my Uzi with the fifty-round clip. "Y'all get down back there. It's only one way out of here and they in the way."

We let them roll up to the shack, and then I saw Juice get out of the Jeep and dust his pants off. Then, about ten other dudes got out with red bandanas around their necks and faces. I figured that my brother was deeply plugged into the Bloodz out of Memphis now. I ain't have no problem with them, or no Bloodz at all, but I figured that if they were under his authority, they had been given the order to kill me and Princess on sight. That made them my enemies because I was gone protect my home-front by any means.

Juice stopped and turned a bottle of Bacardi up, taking long swallows. Then he threw the bottle on the ground and it shattered. He and his crew got to walking toward the shack. At first, it looked like they wasn't gone pay no attention to my whip. But then one of his homies, some fat dude with a bald head, pointed at our car, which made Juice pause and look our way.

As soon as he did, I started the engine, and Princess stuck her Tech out the window. "This what fuck niggas get," she pulled on the trigger.

Datta! Datta! Datta! Datta! Datta! Daaaat!

I stepped on the gas as I saw the fat dude's face explode, and his man that walked alongside of him get hit in the neck. Juice fell to the ground and pulled out a handgun.

Bocka! Bocka! Bocka! Bocka!

Sssssh! The glass to the back window shattered and Jahliya started screaming at the top of her lungs. I looked into my rearview mirror and I saw my mother cover her up and fall to the floor with her.

"Get us out of here, Taurus!"

I could see Juice and the rest of his goons loading up into their red Jeeps, preparing to chase us, I figured. Princess sat on the window sill of the passenger's side, letting her Tech ride in their direction, while I stormed on the gas. Whipping through the dirt path, and rolling over bushes, the only thing on my mind was getting back to the main road, where I could put the pedal to the floor, and lose those niggas. The last thing we needed was to be in a shootout with all of them.

I don't know how, but one of the Jeeps got real close to us. Princess climbed in the back seat, stuck her Tech out of the window, and let it ride.

Daaaaaaaat! Daaaaaat! Daaaaat!

She shattered their windshield. The Jeep swerved, and then slammed into a tree at full speed, exploding almost immediately. I increased my speed as she climbed back into her seat.

"Let's get them out of here," she said, sliding the Tech back under her seat, and grabbing my Uzi.

I came from off the dirt path and made a hard right, almost slamming into a UPS truck. The car fish tailed and then straightened out. I hit the gas before the truck hit us, and we got away from it just in time. I looked back toward the dirt path and saw that all of the Jeeps had stopped. Juice got out of his and nodded his head, mugging our car.

***

By the next morning, we had switched whips, and was pulling up in front of my cousin, Felicia's, house, where she stayed with her daughter, Mercedes. Out of all of my family that still lived in Chicago, I was closest to her. She had done a five-year bit in the pen for a murder that she didn't commit. And after she got home, her daughter, Mercedes, had been kidnapped. She got her back a about a month after she was taken, but they had both been through a lot. Her and my mother were real close, and I knew that she would protect my family until I figured out a way to get everybody out of the country while me and Princess went at Juice head on. I wanted to cut the head off of the snake now that my father was dead.

Felicia lived way out in Evanston, which was a low key suburban neighborhood outside of Chicago. She'd managed to buy herself a nice big house within a gated community, which I thought was cool.

When I pulled up her long drive way, I saw her front door open up and then my lil' cousin Mercedes' lil' chocolate ass was running to the car with a Dior cheerleading uniform on. She damn near tore the door handle off of the backdoor where my sister was seated.

"Mary, Mary, get out and give me a hug," she hollered, pulling the door wide open.

I could tell that Jahliya was just like me because at hearing all of that noise, she started crying at the top of her lungs until I picked her up and kissed her on the cheek. "It's okay, mama. Daddy know yo cousin got a big mouth. But I got you," I said, serious as hell.

I watched Mary and Mercedes hug before Felicia started to make her way down the drive way in some tight Jordache jeans and a tank top. She was high yellow like my mother, and looked damn near mixed.

"How long I gotta stay here, Taurus?" my mother asked, watching Felicia walk up to the car.

"Just until I can wipe Juice off the face of the earth. Ain't no way in hell I'm finna allow him to hurt one of y'all. So, I gotta take care of my business."

"We. We gotta take care of our business because I ain't lettin' you do nothing without me no more. I mean nothing," Princess said, kissing me on the cheek, then laying her head on my shoulder.

"What about KO? What am I gonna do when they find his body in that shack?"

I shook my head. "Don't worry about that. I'mma let that nigga Juice know that I killed him, and that he next. That way it'll take all the heat off of you. Don't you worry about nothing, you hear me?"

She nodded. "Can you at least kiss me on my lips so I can feel better? I mean, if that's okay wit you, Princess?"

Felicia had knocked on my driver's side window.

"Why y'all still sittin' in the car? I made breakfast and I want y'all to eat before you hit the road again."

I rolled down the window and handed her Jahliya. "Yo, take her and we'll meet y'all in there in one hot second. We just finishing up talking about a few things.

She nodded. "Okay, but don't take too long. The food getting cold."

We watched them walk into the house, leaving me, Princess, and my mother in the car. "For the record, it's cool wit me, Deborah. You can kiss him anytime that you want. After all, you brought him into this world."

I turned around, and my mother grabbed my head, and kissed me on the lips. Hers was still a bit swollen, and that hurt my heart. I was glad my old man was dead. My mother would never have to go through that level of pain again. I sucked on her lips, and then we broke apart. As soon as we did, Princess grabbed her and they started making out. She held my mother by the sides of her head, and they must've kissed for a full two minutes.

"I told you that from now on, you ain't doing nothing without me. If we gone heal our mother, then we gone do it together. That's how that's gone go."

I laughed. "Yeah, mama, I told her everything in regards to you and I. Me and her don't have any secrets."

My mother lowered her head, and Princess reached and lifted her chin back up. "It's okay, mama. My family got secrets, too. Every family do. The bottom line is that I love your son, and I love you for bringing him into this world. You are an amazing woman, and I honor you. I want to heal you just as bad as he does, so for you, anything goes." She kissed her on the lips again.

I felt humbled, and thankful at the same time because it took a special kind of woman to embrace our situation the way that Princess did. I didn't think I could accept her father in the way that she had accepted my mother. I was too selfish and jealous for that. I knew that I would wind up healing my mother again, and the fact that Princess was willing to be in that bed with us made me fall in love with her ass real hard.

At the breakfast table, I got to stuffing my face with French Toast, and forking up one of the cheesiest omelets that I had ever eaten in my life. It was stuffed with Tennessee Pride sausages, and that was my favorite kind. I was chewing so hard that my jaw started to hurt. I had to stop for a second and take a deep breath. Princess reached over and rubbed my face. She had chewed up some of her food and was feeding it to our daughter.

"Baby, I told you I don't want her eating adult food just yet. I don't want my daughter big as a house. She's a girl. She's not ready yet."

Jahliya ate what she was offering to her frowning. She was spitting it back out, and chewing at the same time. Princess waved me off. "Boy, I'm slim, my mother slim, your mother thick wit it, but still nice and slim, your sister slim, what are you worried about?"

I shook my head. "I just want her eating healthy, that's all."

Felicia started laughing. "Y'all don't pay him no attention, he just havin' that first time parent syndrome. He'll be alright after a while."

I didn't know what that was, and I didn't care to ask. I just felt it was better to move on because I was outnumbered by females, and that would make it impossible to win an argument.

Mercedes got up from her seat and wrapped her arm around my shoulder. "Y'all better leave my cousin alone. That's probably why he don't come up here like that." She kissed me on the cheek. "It's okay, cuz. I love you, and I got yo back."

"Lil' girl, if you don't sit yo lil' thick self-down, all over my man like that, I'mma have to cut you," Princess said, laughing, but I knew she was serious because she removed Mercedes' arm from around my shoulder, and sat on my lap possessively.

Mercedes looked at her like she was crazy. "Dang, you one of them types, huh?"

Princess closed her eyes and smiled. "I sure am. This me right here, and I ain't going. I know you his family in all, but you too damn bad with them lil' shorts on. Hell nall."

"I told her she don't know how cold she is. Mercedes think she still a lil' teenager, when the world don't see her like that."

"Mama, please, let's not get into this again," she said, rolling her eyes. "I'm finna go anyway because Mel about to scoop me up and we flyin' out to Vegas for the weekend." She hurried and kissed me on the cheek. "Later, cousin."

Princess looked like she wanted to kill her ass. I could feel her shaking a little bit.

"How long has it been since she's been back?" my mother asked.

"It's been almost six months, and we been pressing forward. Just one day at a time. They still don't know where Kelli at. I can't believe she killed them girls like that, and Ron."

"Dang, forgot about him. That's sad. That lil' girl ain't have a chance, though. It's no wonder she was all screwed up in the head. How was you able to buy this house?"

"Before Ron died, he wrote these books called Unforgivable Sins. It's four of them, and I been living off them royalty checks. They just turned the first book into a movie, and I'm thinking, since it's four of them, they might do it with every single one. Fingers crossed."

"What is the books about?"

"Our whole story is in there, mines, Mercedes', Ron's, and Kelli's. Them some of the coldest books I ever read, and they all are factual."

"Damn, here they go right here at Amazon. I'm finna order all four of them so I can know what's going on."

Felicia nodded. "That's what's up. Anyway, Deborah, you can stay here for as long as you need to. Don't nobody know where I am, and I wanna keep it that way."

I slid her a ten-thousand-dollar knot across the table. "That's you right there. It ain't got nothin' to do wit what you doin' fo' my people. It's just because you so thorough, and I love you like crazy."

That night, me and Princess set out to leave town. We were walking back to the car when my mother ran out and into my arms.

"Baby, please, can y'all heal me before you go. I need it so bad. I'll do anything."

Our hotel room door at the Hilton was barely closed before Princess attacked my mother, walking her backward into the wall, taking her skirt and pulling it above her hips, before sliding her hand down her panties.

"Ummm, baby, do you," she moaned, and spread her legs apart.

I popped the cork out of the bottle of Patron and turned it up. Sitting on the love seat that overlooked the bed, I had the perfect view.

"I ain't gone even lie, mama, you been fine to me. I wish I would have grown up in the house with you. I would have made you give me a bath every night," Princess moaned as my mother sucked allover her neck, and stuck her hand into her panties. It started moving back and forth and Princess' eyes rolled into the back of her head.

"Ummm yes, mama, that feels so good."

My mother dropped to her knees and pulled Princess' panties down her thighs and off, but not before licking the crotch of them. That shit turned me on, and I was now starting to understand why I was so damn freaky.

When she stood back up, Princess dropped down and pulled off her panties. My mother spread her legs, and Princess stuck her face right in between them, slurping so loud that my dick started throbbing. I had to pull it out and stroke it some. I made eye contact with my moms, and she licked her lips, and mouthed the words "thank you" before closing her eyes and leaning her head back.

When she got to making all of those loud sex noises, my body started to get amped up. I walked over to them with my dick sticking out in front of me and picked up Princess, throwing her on the bed. Then I picked my mother up, and she wrapped her legs around me, sliding down on my meat. When it entered her hot oven, I damn near came right away. She screamed in my ear as I bounced her up and down, holding on to her ass. That pussy was good and tight. It was wet and gripping me at every stroke, driving me crazy.

"Lay her down, daddy, so I can suck on her pretty titties. I wanna be her baby for a minute."

I laid her on her back, and started to ram that pussy long and hard while she cried. "I love you, baby. I love you so much. Don't nobody love me like you doooooo! Un uhhhh, baby, I'm cominnn'," she started to arch her back and scream while I continued to dig into her at full speed. Then Princess was sucking on her pearl tongue, and that drove her through the roof.

Next, her and Princess 69'd while I rubbed their asses, and drank from the bottle of Patron. It ended with us having a threesome in the Jacuzzi. We fucked all the way until the sun started to peek over the horizon. Before we all fell out, my mother hugged us close.

"I love y'all so much, and thank you."

Chapter 8

"Taurus, wake up! Wake up! That nigga Juice just cut up my aunty in Orange Mound," Princess screamed into my ear.

I shot out of the bed like somebody was chasing me. At first my brain didn't register what she'd said. I didn't get why Juice would go all the way to New Jersey just to body her aunty. "Baby, what are you talking about?" By that time my mother was awake and looking at us like she was terrified.

"My Aunty Rose, my mother's sister. You know, the one that Pac Man stayed with. Her daughter just hit me up on Facebook and told me that she found her mother chopped up into pieces when she got home from work, and that nigga Juice was parked outside her house with two other Jeeps. He told her to tell me to get at him, and that his father's blood was gone drown us."

I ain't know what to say. I really ain't have no kind of real relationship with her aunty, so I ain't feel no type of way, just keeping shit real. I mean, we had our daughter back. My mother and sister were safe. I ain't feel like avenging her aunt's death.

"Baby, so what, was you close to her or something?" I asked, walking to the shower. My mother followed me, and went into the bathroom ahead of me. I could hear the shower water running.

Princess sat on the bed and placed her hands over her face. She inhaled and then exhaled loudly. "Ahhh! This nigga been a thorn in my fucking side since day one. Kilt my brother, took my daughter, and now he done killed my aunty." She took her hands away from her face and eyed me with a look on her face that said she was ready to get even. "When are we gon' kill this nigga? I mean, why are we waiting around for him to keep picking off pieces of us. How dumb can we be?"

I walked over to her and knelt down. "I'm ready to body this nigga, too. Trust me, ma. But we gotta be smart. We can't get to doing shit the wrong way, or we gone wind up in the pen like Tywain. Then who gone protect our family?"

We all showered together, and after dropping my mother off, me and Princess hit the road and wound up in Memphis early the next day. We met up with her cousin, Jill, at the Greyhound bus station. She had a black hoodie on, and some black jogging pants. She looked like she was ready to rob a bank. She got in the back of our rental, and started talking a mile a minute.

"I ain't call the police, just like y'all told me not to. When you go in the house, you gone find her in the kitchen in a hundred pieces. It's blood everywhere. When I first saw it I passed out, and I hit you up right away. I'm so glad you picked up, too, because I didn't know what to do. I gotta get out of here. But where I'm gone go? I know Juice looking for me now. But then again, why would he be? Probably cause he crazy. Yeah, I'm out of here." She threw some keys at Princess and they hit her shoulder and fell on the floormat. She opened the back door, prepared to get out.

"Damn Jill, wait a minute before you go running off," Princess said, opening the driver's side door and getting halfway out to stop her.

Jill pulled out a pack of Newport shorts, and popped one in her mouth, lighting the tip. "I'm so fucking scared, Princess, that I don't know what to do. Juice got every blood in Memphis running behind his crazy ass. They worship him like he some type of God, and I don't know why." She lowered her head. "Why would he kill my mother, though? Why?" she fell to her knees and broke down crying.

Princess opened the backdoor, and helped her to get into it. There were about twenty people around and they were looking at us like we were crazy. Princess slid in the backseat with her and put her arm around Jill's shoulder. "It's gonna be alright, Jill. We finna find that nigga and body his ass. He not gone get away with this, trust me."

"That ain't gone bring my mama back, Princess," she whimpered and cried into her shoulder. "I just don't understand. My mother ain't did nothing wrong to nobody. For him to kill her in the way that he did is just sick."

"Are you sure that you didn't tell nobody about this?" Princess asked, pulling Jill away from her so she could look into her eyes.

"Unless somebody saw what I wrote to you on Facebook. Other than that, I haven't said nothing to nobody out here."

I pulled out ten hundred-dollar bills and gave them to her. "Look, this a gee right here. It ain't much, but it's all the cash I got on me right now. Take this and leave the city. Let me and Princess find this nigga, and make him pay for his sins. She'll let you know when it's good to come back, then we can bury your mother and give her the respects that she need. We'll foot the bill. I know it ain't much, but considering the circumstances."

She nodded with tears cascading down her cheeks. "I wish your brother was like you, Taurus. I wish he had some sort of human decency in him. I mean, wait until you see what he did to my mother. Just wait." She broke down crying again, and Princess rubbed her back.

***

We went in through the back door, and entered into a hallway that led to the kitchen. As soon as we got about twenty feet away from the scene, I could smell that horrible stench that came from dead bodies. It didn't help that the heat was on in their crib. It felt like it was ninety degrees in that house, and I could only imagine that it added to the body decomposing as fast as it was. It smelled like boiled cats. I mean, it smelled so horrible that I could barely breathe.

"Yo, it smells bad as fuck in here," Princess said, going into a fit of coughs. I had to lightly tap her on the back while we continued on to the kitchen. As soon as we got to the doorway, I could see blood all over the refrigerator because the hallway ran right into the refrigerator. And when we turned left, we were officially in the kitchen. Right there on the floor was about a hundred rats, and a million roaches, crawling all over the chopped off body parts of Princess's aunty.

"Oh my God," she exclaimed. "Look at all this shit."

The rats were making little screeching sounds and gnawing away with blood on their mouths. The roached crawled everywhere, and the whole scene made me itch. Juice had cut her head off and sat it on the stove with a knife on the top of it. Her eyes were wide open, and there were two rats eating at her cheeks. One of her arms was on the side of the stove being worked on by three rats, and a hundred roaches. We found one of her legs in the sink with three rats eating away at it.

And her torso on the side of the refrigerator with ten rats gnawing away at that. The whole scene was more than Princess could handle. Her jaws blew out, and she looked like she was getting ready to puke. I hurried and grabbed the garbage can, and she threw up in it.

"Baby, let's get the fuck out of here. Ain't nothing we can do for her right now."

***

"Yo, Taurus, I need you to roll over to the Mound. That nigga Deion just got hit up by them Blood niggas," Gary said, hollering into the phone.

Gary was one of Tywain's lil' homies we had moving our heroin for us. He was a street nigga, with crazy street smarts. He'd been in the gutta his whole life, and all he knew was hustle. Deion was in charge of moving cocaine out in Orange Mound. He was just as down as Gary, but way crazier when it came to that pistol play. I had love for both of the lil' niggas, including Martell who we had fucking around in that Meth game. Every one of them played a crucial role to us. Me and Tywain were knee deep in the game, but we weren't the types to sit in a spot all day, or answer a phone to collect paper. We collected from their hard work. That's how most niggas wanted to have it, and we did. They each had their own workers, and they worked for us. It was a Pyramid of which me and Tywain sat on the top.

When we pulled up in Orange Mound, Gary and about five young niggas walked up to the car and stood outside of it until I got out. There were police everywhere. It looked like somebody had just got raided. People were all outside in their house shoes and night gowns, being nosey. Little kids were huddled up, probably telling their own version of what they thought happened, and there were groups of grown folks, doing the same thing, I imagined.

I got out and gave Gary a half a hug. "Yo, it gotta be that nigga Juice, mane," he said with a real strong country drawl.

He was really dark skinned with a mouth full of gold, and kinda heavy set.

I looked around and felt uncomfortable. Me and Princess had been doing so much dirt that I wondered if we were on the police's radar. "Oh yeah, lil' homie, what make you say that?"

"That nigga pulled up on me last night, rolled his window down, and pointed an assault rifle at my chest while I was walking wit my baby mama. Nigga said, 'I should kill you right in front of that bitch and that punk ass kid. Any nigga fuck wit Taurus is an enemy of me and my father.'" He wiped some sweat away from his forehead. "That nigga was about to kill us, mane had the 12's not rolled down the block when they did. I can bet on nat. And I ain't never had no problems wit blood."

"Yea, we Bloods like that nigga. Fuck they aimin' at the fam for?" asked another fat dude with plenty jewelry around his neck. "I been fam since I was nine years old. This some new shit right here, mane."

Four more Police cars rolled up, and the officers stepped out of their cars, looking over at our group.

"Baby, you see how they lookin' over here?" Princess asked, starting up the car. "Yo, let's get the fuck out of here. If that nigga Deion lean ain't nothin' we can do about it."

"Hold on. What you talking about lean, shorty? Homie ain't dead, he just shot up a little bit. My nigga gone pull through. We been through worse," Gary said, looking over his shoulder.

There were six police officers on their way over to where we were standing. "Yo, I'mma get up wit you in a minute

Gary. Twelve on they way over here, and I ain't about to answer no questions about shit." I got into the car, and Princess started to pull away from the curb.

"I got about two hundred fifty gees for you nigga, so we need to meet up," Gary said, walking away from where he and his homies previously stood.

I did the *I'mma call you* sign wit my fingers and put it to my ear. I saw him nod before two police officers blocked his path with a writing pad in their hand.

***

"Yo, how you been in here, boss?" I asked Tywain as soon as he picked up the phone on the other side of the glass. He looked like he was getting bigger, like either he'd been pumping plenty iron or just eating good.

"I can't really complain. I'm just ready to break this seal doe." He switched the phone from one ear to his other one. "I hear that nigga Juice out there causing hell. Yo, old man got kilt?" he asked raising an eyebrow.

"Yeah, it's plenty shit that done took place that's been crazy. But the bottom line is that that fool goin' on a rampage ever since he got out. I think all that dope he doin' startin' to fuck wit his mind real bad."

Princess grabbed the phone from me and rolled her eyes. "Since you ain't gon' let me say hi. Damn, y'all act like I ain't sittin' here, too." She looked at Tywain and curled her upper lip. "What you can't speak to me no more or somethin'?"

I could see his mouth moving, but couldn't hear what he was saying. He did start laughing, and then nodded his head.

"I would show you my titties but these days Taurus been on some possessive shit. But if he say it's cool, then I will." She gave me a look that said she wanted to know my answer.

"If you wanna show the homie yo titties, that's up to you. I ain't got nothin' to do wit that," I said. It bothered me a little bit but I ain't wanna seem like a wimp in front of my nigga. Plus, if I was on lock and he brought his BM up and she was willing to show me her titties, I would definitely wanna see 'em, and do my thing while she played wit 'em. So, I ain't say shit.

"Okay, so you sayin' it's cool then, because yo nigga wanna jag his dick while he look at my titties, and I'm gonna do it because he's yo nigga. But if you don't want me to, I won't because I'm supposed to be yo woman. So, tell me what to do."

Tywain got to beating on the glass and she handed me the phone. I grabbed it, and shook my head at her crazy ass. "What's good fool?"

"I know that's yo baby mama and all, but I'm tryna see some shit, nigga. I ain't busted in damn near a month. I need to get right. Let me see what she workin' wit."

"Yo, it's good, Princess. Let him see 'em." I stood up and threw the deuces at the homie. I was going to leave so he could do his thing to her.

"Wait, baby, he sayin' somethin' to you."

I grabbed the phone. "Whut up, bro?"

"Make sure you go check on my daughter today when y'all leave here, man. I been trying to call my sister, and she ain't been picking up. Neither is my aunt, or my uncle, and that ain't right. So, touch bases wit them for me, and I appreciate it. Oh, and you ain't gotta send me no cash for a minute. I got damn near two hundred gees on my books fuckin' wit you. That don't look right. You know how Tennessee get down."

"A'ight, I got you, kid. Is it anything else you need for me to do?" I asked, looking over to Princess who held her head down as if she was sick.

"Yeah, take your BM home. She sick right now 'cuz you was finna let her show me them titties. She might act like she really hard, but deep down she still a woman. You gotta understand that, or you gon' lose her. So, make it seem like it was your idea to break that shit up, and watch how she respond. Love fool."

"Love, my nigga."

I gave Princess back the phone. She looked up at me like she was drained. Like she was ready to break down crying.

"Baby, say yo goodbyes to the homie, then let's go. If you show that nigga my titties I'm gon' whoop yo ass. You belong to me, and I ain't sharin' you wit no nigga. Period!"

She jumped up and wrapped her arms around my neck. "I love you so much, daddy. I thought you didn't care about me at first. Damn you had me sick."

As she hugged my neck, I looked over at Tywain and he mouthed the words, "I told you."

***

"Bitch ass nigga, ain't you Juice brother?" some lil' young dude said as I was hugged up behind Princess while she stopped in the middle of the grocery store aisle to look over the cereal. The young nigga had on a puffy black coat. He unzipped it and came up with a .380, aiming it right at my chest.

I looked to my right and then my left. There were people shopping everywhere. I couldn't believe that this lil' nigga had enough balls to just pull out his pistol and aim it at me like it was the most normal thing in the world. "Nah, I don't even know who Juice is lil' homie."

He squinted his eyes. "You a muthafucking lie." He stepped forward. "That nigga Juice got twenty gees on yo head dead or alive, and I need that money. I don't usually fuck wit Blood niggas, cuz, but money is green, and I bang for that green."

Princess dropped the box of Trix cereal, and rushed in front of me. "Bitch ass nigga, you betta gone wit that lil' ass gun. You ain't about to do shit to my man. Word is bond!" She mugged the shit out of him.

"Bitch, I'll kill you, too. He got twenty gees on you just as well. You must be that Lil' Queen, or Princess, bitch everybody talking about." He cocked back the .380. "So now that's forty gees."

I tried to pull Princess behind me, but she wasn't going.

"Nall, fuck that. If you gone shoot us, shoot then. But make sure you kill both of us because I'm telling you lil' boy, if you leave one of us alive, word is bond, we killin' you and yo whole family."

"Hey, what are you doing to those people back there?" the store manager yelled.

As soon as he did, the little boy, who couldn't have been older than fourteen, looked over his shoulder. I used that as a distraction and rammed our shopping cart with all of my might into his chest. I mean, I slammed it so hard that I rolled over him, and fell on the floor.

Princess kicked him in the mouth, and helped me get up.

I don't know what his little ass was taking, or if he was human, but he got up bussing.

Boo-wa! Boo-wa! Boo-wa! Boo-wa!
I heard the bullets zipping past us. I made sure that she was blocked by my body as we ran out of that aisle with him chasing us.

People dropped to the floor and some women began screaming at the top of their lungs. Me and Princess ran right, and ended up in the produce section. I got to pulling oranges and apple barrels off their stands, making it so they fell all over the floor. I don't know what the fuck I thought I was doing, because he kept right on bussing.

Boo-wa! Boo-wa!

We ran into the back of the supermarket, where the employees got changed, and the bathrooms were. As soon as we got back there, we saw two women kneeling down with their hands over their head. I grabbed Princess' hand and led her into the bathroom, locking the door behind us.

The little boy kicked it twice, and then bussed again.

Boo-wa! Boo-wa!

"You muthafuckas can't run. Open this mafuckin' door!"

I hoisted Princess up to the only window in the bathroom. She caught the ledge and climbed out of it. Then I jumped up and struggled to do the same. As soon as I got through it, he busted through the door, bussing. *Boo-wa! Boo-wa!* H damn near hit me in the leg.

"Come on, baby," Princess said, running full speed down the alley. She had come out of her wedges, and was running barefoot.

I caught up to her quick, and we ran all the way around to our car that was still in the lot. Just as we got to it, there were about fifty police cars pulling up, and the officers ran inside of the grocery store.

Chapter 9

Gary put the duffle bag of money into the back of my car and slammed the door. "Yo, that's two hundred seventy-five thousand right there. I'm ready for some new product. That nigga Meech hit me up about two hours ago and said he ready for us to meet up. I'm thinking we cop a fresh fifty bricks of that Rebirth and move some of this shit out to Black Haven. We'll get the regular two hundred when Hood Rich get back, he say. No matter what, I'll need about two hundred birds even before next week is out. This shit flying off like hot cakes." He put his hand in the window and we shook up.

"That's what's good. I know I gotta touch bases wit Hood Rich real soon. My mind just been on other shit right now. But it's good that I can trust you to hold shit down."

"Loyalty is everything, big homie. You already know that. I swear by this shit in blood." He beat on his chest.

"How Deion doing?" I asked, lowering my voice to show sympathy. I hated that I hadn't been to the hospital to check on him, but I was trying to get my bearings. That nigga Juice had to go.

He shook his head. "Not good, bro. They sayin' the homie might not make it out of the week."

"Damn. I'm sorry to hear that, lil' homie."

We were silent for a lil' while. He took out a Visine bottle and turned it upside down. He squeezed on it a little bit until a drip appeared, then snorted it up his nose. First one nostril, and then the other one. "It's the life we live out here, mane. It's fuck niggas everywhere you go. But what we gone do about hat nigga Juice, mane?"

Princess laughed out loud. "He livin' on borrowed time. Trust me on that one. His luck gon' run out sooner or later."

I nodded. "Every day we out here looking for that nigga, bro. He can only hide for so long."

"Yeah, mane, well let me know when we gone shut down shop for the week so we can go looking for this fuck nigga. I wouldn't mind losing a few dollas if it mean we gone body that clown ya under, dig me?" he said, snorting the drips from the Visine bottle again.

I knew from experience that he'd applied heroin to the water in the Visine bottle, and it was a new way of snorting the drug.

"Say, Gary, don't tell me you snortin' that Rebirth?"

He wiped his nose and snorted loudly. "Yeah, mane. I mean, how many mafuckas you know work at McDonald's and don't eat the food?" He closed his eyes, and then opened them back after wiping his mouth with his hand. Behind him was the expressway. We were in the parking lot of a liquor store right outside Black Haven. I got this shit under control though, baby. I ain't came up short yet. Have I?"

I shook my head. "Yo, remember this shit sealed in blood. You fuck up and that's yo ass, my nigga."

"I wouldn't expect that shit to be no other way." He took a cigarette from behind his ear, and lit it.

I watched a little girl ride her bike over to him. She had long pig tails, and looked like she was about eleven or twelve years old at the most. She rolled right up to him and stopped. "Gary, can I have five dollars?" she asked looking up at him and shielding her eyes from the sun.

"Now what you need five dollars fo', Punkin? Every time I see you, you want some money." He laughed going into his pocket. He pulled out a knot so fat that it looked like a folded dictionary.

A green Yukon Denali pulled into the lot. I couldn't see who was in the truck because they were behind mirror tints, but I got to feeling weird like.

"Daddy, you see that truck just roll up?" Princess asked, putting the Uzi on her lap. "My Spider senses going off right now."

"Yeah, I see it." I cocked the Mach .10 and put it on my lap, waiting for the occupants to get out of the truck, or to show themselves in any way. "Yo, Gary, you see that truck over there that just rolled in?"

He looked over his shoulder. "Yeah. What's good wit them though?"

Just when they started to get out of the truck, something told me to look to my left. When I did, I damn near jumped out of my seat. The little girl had dropped her bike to the ground. She came out of her capris with a Gauge, slammed it into Gary's stomach, and pulled the trigger, blowing a hole through him.

Bloom!

His muscles and tissues splashed across my face and into the car. Somehow, he managed to turn around and she hit him again.

Bloom!

This time the bullet ripped through his neck and twisted him in the air before he fell on top of our car's hood.

Princess leaned over me and pulled her trigger. "You lil' dirty bitch!"

Bap! Bap! Bap! Bap!

She hit the little girl all up and down her body, knocking chunks of meat off of her before she laid leaking on the concrete.

Bloom! Bloom! Bloom!

Our windshield shattered, and I saw that the truck had opened its doors and the occupants were shooting at us, to kill. I raised the Mach and, at the same time, hit the gas, sending our car speeding backward.

Vrrrrrr. Vrrrr. Vrrrrr.

I busted, sending hot lead at they ass, but not hitting nobody. They ducked down and kept busting their shot guns.

Bloom. Bloom. Bloom. Bloom. Bloom.

Eeeeerrr, I skidded out of the parking lot, and a car slammed into my back-passenger's door. The driver jumped out of the car busting.

Boom. Boom. Boom.

Princess ducked down, and I did the same thing. Stepping on the gas and speeding down the side street. I almost hit some little boys that were in the middle of the street throwing their football back and forth. I didn't understand why they didn't run when they heard the gun shots.

Princess stuck her head out of the window and aimed her Tech at the car that was speeding fast behind us.

Bap. Bap. Bap.

Her bullets jumped from the gun and released the shell casings. I could smell the gunpowder, and it excited me. "Bitch ass niggaz!"

"Fuck this shit, boo. Mafuckas think it's sweet." I slammed on the brakes and the car smashed into us loudly. As if we were both thinking the same thing, we swung open our doors and let they ass have it.

Bap. Bap. Bap. Vrrrrr. Vrrr. Vrrrr.

Our bullets chopped up their car and shattered the windshield, causing blood to spray across it before it caved in. I jumped on the top of the hood, while Princess ran around to the passenger side, and let her weapon go. The driver was ducked down with a red rag on his face. Bleeding all over the back. I aimed and pulled the trigger. Vrrr. He shook before leaning over to the side. Meanwhile, Princess finger fucked that Tech again and again. We rocked their car, jumped back in ours, and I smashed off.

The shooting was all over the news, and so were our pictures. They had a few good shots of us, especially since they traced us back to being at the grocery store. I sat there on the couch in her cousin's basement shaking my head.

Princess paced back and forth. "What the fuck is we gon' do? What are we gon' do?" she asked with a fat ass blunt in her hand. It looked like a regular cigar before you took the tobacco out.

"I don't know, but we gotta find that nigga Juice and get the fuck outta here."

"Find Juice? Nigga, we got the whole Tennessee looking for our ass. Tryna find Juice gon' get us popped." She plopped down on the couch.

My phone vibrated. I looked at the face and saw that it was Juice's line. He wanted to Facetime. "Here go that nigga Juice right here."

Princess looked over my shoulder. "Yo, see what's good."

"What's good, nigga? Where you at?" I asked, standing up.

Princess stood up with me, and made me lower the phone by pulling my arm down. "I can't see."

Juice had a red rag over his face, but I could tell it was him by the eyes. "The question ain't where I am, the question is who the fuck is this?" He held up Tywain's daughter by her hair. She screamed, and cried. "This lil' bitch right here is about to lose her life, and it's all because of you. Fucked up, ain't it? She aint even one yet." He threw her on the ground.

The next thing I knew he dropped to his knees and brought a hammer down into the kid's face again and again. The first blow stuck into the child's head. He wiggled it, and then brought it down again, smashing the face. Blow after blow until the baby's head was flat against the concrete. He got back into the camera breathing hard. "Blood in, Blood out, my nigga. See me!"

***

I must have had a death wish or something, because the next morning I went to see Tywain with a dope head's ID. I had to tell the homie in person what had happened to his daughter. And even though Princess damn hear kilt me to try and stop me from going, I went anyway.

Tywain threw the phone against the window and broke down to his knees. I watched him through the glass rock back and forth, and it crushed my soul. That was my right-hand man, and had been ever since I'd gotten to Memphis and we whooped some niggas in school together. My A-1 since day one.

I adjusted the big fake beard on my face, and tried to get a little more comfortable under the fake dreads on my head. I looked around and people were doing their own things. I was glad, because I couldn't stand the heat.

He slowly crawled back up to the phone. "Yo, my baby ain't never had a chance, man. That's why I should have kilt that nigga Juice back in the day." Tears dropped from his eyes. "Yo, but I know where he layin' his head, though." He sniffed snot back into his nostrils. "One of the lil' Blood niggas that I grew up wit in here. He caught a body over on Port Washington. He say that nigga Juice sent him off, and he heated. Long story short, you remember that bitch Mardi that Juice bumped at that roller skating place down in Houston when yo pops went to meet Jerry Walker for the first time?"

I nodded. "Yeah, you talkin' about that Mexican bitch wit the fat ass booty."

He nodded. "Yeah, he got her ducked off in Stoughton. They got a crib on the east side, and I got the address from lil' homie. Yo, kill that nigga for me, Blood. Torture that fuck nigga and make him pay."

Princess seemed like she was so anxious to kill Juice that, when I told her where he was laying his head, she damn near fell out of the tub trying to get dressed.

"Damn, ma, at least dry yourself off before you put that nun shit back on," I said, putting on my nun costume. We figured that it was the only way for us to move about without being spotted, and it was her idea.

"Fuck this water, I'm ready to body this nigga so we can get a move on."

Two hours later, we pulled up in the back of Juice's duck off spot. He had the nerve to move out to the suburbs in a real nice neighborhood. The nigga had a gate around his house, and the grass was cut all nice and neat. The bushes were shaped, and it just blew my mind.

First thing Princess said when we rolled up and confirmed that it was the house was, "aw hell nall. I'm definitely burning this mafucka down before we leave. Ain't no way in hell this nigga deserve a spot like this. She twisted the noise reduction system onto the barrel of her M.90, and I did the same to mine.

It held one hundred twenty shots in the magazine, and I had two more of them in my back pocket. I tightened my vest, and made sure that she did the same.

"I don't wanna wear this hot ass vest, Taurus. If it's my time, then I'm ready to go. This mafucka is so uncomfortable." she said, sticking her finger into the arm hole to scratch her chest.

"Once again, I'm daddy. And I want my baby girl protected as much as possible. So that's that."

"Okay, daddy," she said, kissing me on the cheek.

We crept around the side of the house, looking for a window that would potentially be open. It wasn't that hot outside so I didn't think that they'd have all of them closed to run their A/C. So, I looked to see if any window was cracked, but couldn't find one. We had previously thought about going in from the back way, but he had three big ass Doberman Pinschers in the backyard, so that killed that.

"So, what we gon' do?" Princess asked, crouching down next to me on the side of his house.

"I'm ready to kick that mafuckin' doe in. I ain't got time for this shit. "I stood up and started to walk to the front of the house just as the wind picked up, and the temperature dropped.

"Shid, it works for me," Princess said, probably just ready to wet some shit.

The Angel of Death must have been smiling up at us because, when we got to the front of the house, there was a pizza delivery man knocking on the door. I was so happy that I turned and kissed Princess on the forehead.

She grabbed my dick. "I'm sucking the skin off of this ma-fucka tonight, I can promise you that," she said, and cocked the M.90. We waited until the front door opened up, and as soon as it did, I hopped over the banister and ran full speed, scooping the fat delivery driver, and running him into the house, where we crashed into Mardi, knocking her backward.

Princess jumped over us and ran into the house, snatching Mardi up and putting the barrel of the gun into her mouth.

"Bitch, you bet not scream because, if you do, I'mma blow yo head clean the fuck off yo shoulders."

I closed the door, wrapped my arm around the delivery driver's neck, and put him in the sleeper hold until he passed out. Then I threw him in the closet that was right by the door.

"Bitch, where is Juice at?" Princess hollered, looking around the house while I held Mardi by the neck against the wall.

"He ain't here. I swear to god, he isn't," she whined.

"Well tell us who all is here, and you bet not leave nobody out," I said, tightening my grip. Even though I knew we was on business, it was still hard for me to be choking her like that. I just didn't like abusing women. I loosened my grip.

"It's just me here. That's it. Juice said he'd been back in the morning. I haven't heard from him since this afternoon. Please don't kill me. I'll tell you where everything is. You can have it all. There has to be more than four hundred thousand dollars, and plenty of dope. Just please don't take my life. I'm pregnant!"

That was common sense. Her belly stood out in front of her like she'd swallowed a watermelon. Princess walked up to her and smacked her so hard across the face that she yelped out in pain. Blood appeared at the corners of her mouth.

"Take me to the money, bitch. Now!" She grabbed her by the hair and threw her in front of us to lead the way.

I opened the closet door, pulled out the delivery man, and twisted my arm around his neck, squeezing with all of my might and pulling upward while I hunched over him. His body started to jerk and I squeezed tighter until he started shaking and kicking his foot.

"I'm sorry, homie, but you a casualty of war. May Jehovah have mercy on yo soul." I wrapped my legs around his body and fell to the floor with him, choking him until he stopped moving. I pushed him back into the closet, and closed the door, jogging to catch up with Princess and Mardi.

When I got into the room, there were stacks of money all over the bed, and Mardi was throwing more out of the safe while Princess aimed her gun at her. "Hurry up, bitch, you takin' too long. Move that big ass belly. Let's go," she demanded.

After she emptied out the safe, I wrapped all the money in a sheet. "Yo, you sure this all this nigga got here?"

"No, there's another safe, but it's full of dope. If you just give me a second, I'll open it for you," she whimpered with tears in her eyes.

Princess grabbed her by the hair. "Bitch, you can keep them crocodile tears to yourself because I feel Nuth'*thing*! I don't give a fuck about you bein' pregnant. I don't give a fuck about you cryin'. And I don't feel some type of way about killin' you." She pulled her hair even tighter. "Yo man out here every single day fuckin' over families, killin' innocent people, and comin' home layin' up wit you. Every bitch know what they man do, and you had to know how yo nigga got down before you became his bottom bitch. So Facetime that nigga. Now!"

She crawled across the floor and did what Princess told her to do. "Juice, please save me," she said into the camera about a minute later.

By that time, we'd pulled the masks over our faces, and I held Mardi in the full Nelson. "Juice, you bitch ass nigga, two can play at this game. You hurt our daughter, killed my brother, and hurt a whole bunch of innocent people. Now you think you about to bring another you in this world?" Princess said holding the phone so he could see his pregnant girl and me holding her. "Well I got news for you."

She handed me the phone and I put it at the perfect angle.

"Aye. Aye. You bitch. Leave my bitch alone. She got my baby in her. I ain't fuck wit y'all daughter. Aye," he hollered into the phone.

Princess rolled her head around on her neck, and then swung and stabbed Mardi right in the chest with a scalpel. She dug the scalpel deep into her, and then pulled it downward, slicing through her stomach.

She screamed, as the blood poured from her mid-section.

Princess stuck her hand into her middle and pulled open the incision until the big ass baby popped out. She held it up, bloody and slimy, by the back of its neck. It looked to be about 28 weeks. The baby started kicking and squirming in her hand.

"You see this shit, Juice? This what the fuck you done turned us into," she shouted with blood dripping from the baby.

Mardi collapsed against me, but I kept on holding her up with a big ass smile on my face. "This bitch falling out, ma, you gotta hurry up."

Juice started screaming like a bitch, "Ahhhhh. You mutha-fuckas. Ahhhh. I'mma kill y'all." The feed went black.

Princess dropped the baby and it bounced off the floor, and then stayed in a slippery mess with its eyes wide open, blink-ing.

I snapped Mardi's neck, and then turned on the stove, blowing the fire out. I wanted to let the gas seep through the house.

We exited the back door. As soon as we did, the four dogs got to running at us full speed. I didn't even move. Princess got down on one knee and shot one dog after the next. *Erp. Erp. Erp. Erp.* They whined as the bullets ripped into their craniums.

Chapter 10

Princess pushed me against the wall and started sucking on my lips. I grabbed her and picked her up, making her wrap her little legs around me. "Daddy, I need you so fucking bad right now. I need my daddy," she whimpered as I fell to the bed with her, landing between her legs.

Pushing her skirt up to her stomach, I ripped her panties off and threw them against the wall. Pulling down my boxers, I grabbed my dick and stuffed it into her little hole. "Daddy need this pussy too, baby girl. I need my little baby right the fuck now!" My dick slid through her wetness. Her pussy was hot and vibrating. We hadn't had the chance to a shower so it had a nice stench to it. Nothing smelled better to me than my woman's pussy.

Princess ripped her blouse open, exposing her small titties with the big ass nipples. "Let's go, daddy. Kill this shit. You already know how we like to fuck. Don't play no games." She opened her legs wide.

I tried to break my dick off in her. I got to pounding so hard that my hips hurt, smashing into her pussy. It sounded like somebody kept on smacking their hands together. I couldn't help groaning and moaning deep within my throat.

"Unn. Unn. Unn. Fuck me, daddy. Fuck yo Princess. I belong to you and only you. You my daddy. This pussy is yours. Ahhhhh. I'm coming all fuckin' readeeeee," she screamed and got to humping into me from the missionary position.

I wrapped my hand around her neck and squeezed, choking her while I sped up my assault. "You belong to me, baby girl. I'm Daddy now and I'll kill a mafucka over you quick. We ride or die to the death, me and my baby girl!" I pushed her knees to her chest and got to going so hard that I drooled a lil' bit.

"Yes, daddy. Yes, daddy. Oh shit, yes, fuck yo baby girl harder, daddeeeeeee!"

When she started shaking, I got to coming with all of my might, jerking, and everything. Then I flipped her onto her knees and got to smacking that ass while I fucked her hard from the back, playing with that asshole.

"When you gone fuck me there, daddy? When you gone fuck yo Princess in that hole right there? I'm so ready!"

I slid out of her and pushed her to the bed. Spreading her ass, I licked out my tongue, putting big globs of spit in her lil' hole and twirling it around with my tongue. Then I smacked her ass cheeks real hard, and pulled her back to all fours. I finger fucked her pussy and rubbed her juices into her ass before taking my big dick head and sliding deeply into her bowels.

"Oh shit, my daddy fucking me in the ass. My daddy fucking me in the ass," she screamed.

That heat was good, too. She got to bouncing back into me and I was barely keeping up because I was ready to bust. Princess' insides were super hot, and I was loving every minute of it.

When I came, I fell against her and kept on playing with her clitoris while she shook on the bed like she was having a seizure.

Afterwards, we sat in the tub with her head on my chest. "Baby, what got you so riled up?" I asked, kissing on the back of her neck.

"I just love my daddy. I was watching how you killed that bitch, and how we been getting down together, and I don't know, it just turned me all the way on."

"What you mean you love me?" I asked. teasing her, and sliding my tongue in her ear.

"Yeah, yeah, yeah. I do love you." She tried to turn around to face me but couldn't quite make the full one hundred eighty-degree turn. "What, you don't love me or something?"

I laughed. "I mean, you a'ight."

"What?"

I felt her getting out of the tub so I moved backward. She grabbed a towel and wrapped it around her body. I got out of the tub and said fuck a towel. I decided to let my dick hang. I needed to know what was good with her. When I got out of the bathroom, she was sitting on the edge of the bed, putting baby oil on her thighs. I got to feeling some type of way immediately. It was something about her lil' body that drove me crazy.

"What's your problem, Princess?"

She waved me off. "Shut up talking to me, Taurus. Word is bond. "She curled her upper lip and rubbed the baby oil into her calves.

"Who the fuck you think you talking to?"

She shot daggers at me with her eyes. "Nigga, I'm talking to yo big black ass. Now what?" She looked like she wanted to stand up.

"What's yo problem?" I came over to her and knelt down in front of her.

"My problem is that I'm telling you that I love you, and you think this shit is a game. This ain't no fucking game! Don't you know what it means when I say I love you?" she asked standing up and getting in my face.

I stood all the way up and looked down on her. Looking her in the eyes as tears fell from hers, I began to speak, "Yo, man, ma, you my Princess. I love the fuck out of you. You the first female that I ever loved outside of my mother and sister. You're my first and only love. I ain't seein' shit pass you. That's my word."

She blinked tears. "Really, daddy?" She walked into me with her head down, and laid it on my chest. "I love you so fuckin' much that its making me crazy. Can you understand that? I aint never felt this way about a man before. I thought that my father had ruined the part of me that actually emotionally desired a man. Then you come along, and you just changed my mind on so many levels. I don't understand it." I could hear her sobbing under me.

I held her tighter. "How you think I feel? I ain't never tried to stay with a female long enough to develop strong feelings because I always figured that I had inside of me what my ol' man was. I been too scared to fall in love, thinking that once I did, I was gone love the woman so hard that it made me abuse her every single day until I fell out of love with her. I never wanted to hurt no female like that. But I love the fuck out of you, Princess. I mean, I love you more than life itself. Ever since I met you, I been feelin' you. And even though I'm afraid of what's inside of me because of my old man, I'm still gon' take that leap." I turned her around to face me and kissed her forehead before tilting her chin and kissing them juicy lips. "I'll never hurt you on purpose. I'm livin' for you and our daughter right now."

She wrapped her arms around me, and we laid in the bed in silence for about ten minutes. "So, can I release myself into you?" she asked, rubbing my abs.

"Yeah, Princess, you can."

"Taurus, but will you always protect me no matter what? Will I always be safe in your arms?" I could hear her voice breaking up again.

I nodded. "Yeah, boo, until my last breath."

She climbed up my body and laid her head on my chest. "From here on out, I give you my life, and every beat of my heart." She kissed me on the neck. "But I'm tellin' you now that this ain't a game with me. I'm already crazy about yo ass. So, if you decide to wake up one day with changed feelings, that ain't gon' fair well for you, or whoever you decide to play me for."

I rubbed her back. "Princess, I ain't never finna put no-body before you. I'm more of a man than that. The only person that comes second to you is our daughter. Then after her, my mother and sister. But you sit all up on that throne by yourself. I promise you that will never change."

She straddled me and looked down into my face with tears rolling down her cheeks. "I been through a lot, Taurus. I been hurt so much, and so badly by everybody that was supposed to protect me. I been lied to since forever, and I believed those lies. Those are the same lies that have me as crazy as I am right now. So, I don't believe words. And I don't believe peo-ple. If I believe the words that carne out of a person's mouth, that means that I love them, and that I am submissive to only them. To have me believe is to have me gone in the head. But you know what, Taurus?"

"What's that, baby girl?" I asked, placing my hands on her exposed thighs.

"Daddy, I believe you."

That night, we Face Timed our daughter, and stayed up talking to. I kept Princess wrapped in my arms protectively and possessively. We had the entire world against us, it seemed, and I didn't know how long it would be before our time ran out, so I wanted to enjoy every moment of having her in my warm embrace.

"Tell me again why we driving all the way down here? Why we ain't just get on a plane? And lastly, why is we meeting this bitch again?" Princess asked as I increased my speed to seventy miles an hour.

"Baby, we can't stay in Memphis forever. I wanna transition over to Texas, and get money out there. Blaze got a few plugs that I need to sit down wit so we can get some shit in order. So, I need you to just roll wit me for the moment," I said, looking over at her while she looked back at me like my head was on backwards.

"And why we ain't get on a plane?"

"Because we hot as hell right now. They got our pictures up all over the news in Memphis. The last thing we need to do is be stopped at the airport on some dumb shit."

"Oh yea, damn, that do make sense." She smacked me on the arm. "That's what I mean when I say you got my mind all fucked up. Had I been thinking clearly, I would have known that. Damn, love a make you get stupid if you ain't careful." She smiled and sucked on her bottom lip. "I love you though, daddy, and you bet not flex on me for this bitch once we get out here. I mean, you ain't gotta let her know what it is right away, if you usin' her for her connects. But at the same time, you betta give me the respect that I'm owed as bein' your princess, and queen. Do we understand each other?"

I couldn't help laughing. "Chill yo lil' ass out. I got this, and I already told you what it is. Ain't no bitch comin' before you, connects or no connects."

"A'ight, 'cuz you know I ain't gon' have no problem cuttin' that bitch up like I'm editin' her ass."

"Yeah, boo, I know."

***

When I stepped out of the Benz truck, Blaze saw me and got to running at me until she jumped into my arms, once again wrapping her legs around me. "Hey, baby, I missed you so much. I'm so glad you're here? Do you like the truck I bought you? That's Mercedes' newest model. They just released that off the showroom floor."

I kissed her on the cheek, looking over her shoulder into the eyes of Princess as she sat in the truck, glaring at me through the windshield. She put a finger to her neck and slid it across as if to say that she'd kill Blaze. I got the message. Blaze's back was turned to her so she couldn't see the gesture.

Blaze licked my neck. "I want you to fuck me all weekend too, baby. I mean, I want you to put it down like you never have before, so that when you leave, my shit be hurting me. I got so many things arranged for us, but first you gotta meet wit my cousin, Flip."

I put her down. "Look, Blaze, there's something I gotta tell you, and I don't want you acting all funny and shit, because I got this. Just hear me out. Can you do that?"

She looked into my eyes, and placed both of her hands on my chest. "Yeah, baby. What's the matter, and is there anything that I can do to fix it for you?"

I shook my head. "I got Princess wit me and every bit of business that's about to go down, I want her a part of it because while Tywain on lock, she been my right hand, and she damn good at being that. Now I know how you feel about me, and you know I care about you, too. But this is bigger than emotions. I just need for you to understand that, if you really care about me."

She looked over her shoulder and I can only imagine they made eye contact. "Oh, okay, I see what it is." She turned back to me, and bit on her finger nail. "She's not gone stop us from getting down, is she? Because I need you in the worst way, Taurus. Every time I know you're about to meet up with me, my pussy just get so wet. I get to feenin' for you, and I can't keep my juices in. Don't you remember me tellin' you before that I would be able to put up with anything just as long as you stay whippin' that dick on me?"

I nodded. "Yeah, I remember, and nall, she ain't gon' break that up. We got an understandin', so you ain't got nothing to worry about."

***

Blaze sat a big bowl of baked macaroni and cheese on the table. Beside it was southern fried chicken, collard greens, cornbread, pinto beans, and white rice, and she said that in the oven was the nearly finished product of a 7up pound cake. She left back out of the dining room to go and glaze it.

"Yo, I still don't like this pretty ass bitch. Every time she look at you, I notice her nipples start poking through that Givenchy Dress. This bitch makin' me wanna stuff her into that oven with the cake," Princess said, mugging the back of Blaze's head as she walked back into the kitchen.

"Chill out, ma. I just need you to be smooth for a few days. Take a break from bodying shit so we can get some business handled out here," I said, squeezing her thigh under the table.

"Yeah, a'ight, I guess I'll try, but I ain't making you no promises."

Blaze came back in and sat a bottle of Tabasco sauce on the table. I could feel my mouth salivating. "My cousin just text me and said he right down the street, so I'm gon' go and open the door." She took the apron from around her waist, and I couldn't help eyeing that big ass ghetto booty. That mafucka was sticking through that dress like a pregnant belly.

I had to shake my head to get those crazy thoughts out of my head. I looked over at Princess and she was mugging the shit out of me.

"Yeah, I think I'mma have to kill that bitch before it's all said and done."

Flip was about six feet ten inches tall, with long corn rows. He had a lil' size on him, too. I guess, back in the day, he had been a rapper, or whatever, and put Clover City on the map. I had never heard of him, but Blaze made sure that was the first thing she said while we were shaking up.

His mans, Screw, was chubby, with a mouth full of gold, and a low haircut. He looked like he was about five feet nine. I couldn't really get a particular vibe from either of them. But I was definitely trying to find one.

After we washed our hands, I got to fucking that food up. I mean, I wasn't playing no games. With all of the hustling and bustling that me and Princess had been doing, we'd been neglecting our stomachs. I watched her grab a piece of chicken and rip it apart with her teeth like a hungry lion.

Flip laughed. "That's right, shawty, eat that shit. That's one thing I find attractive in a woman is if you don't be actin' all shy when it come time to throw down. That's what's up."

Screw mixed his rice and beans together, then crushed the cornbread over it. "Blaze, you be throwing down in that kitchen. You remind me of my mama."

She smiled. "Thank you, Screw. Just as long as you like everything. I put my heart in it, so it should be good."

"Well, girl, it show taste like love to me," Princess said, smacking so loud that I wanted to push her out her chair. She stuffed her mouth with a big piece of cornbread, burped, and started smacking again. "It's been a long time since I had a meal this good. I definitely gotta give you yo props. Don't mean that I like you, but I show love your food."

I inhaled deeply and mugged the shit out of her. "She just playing, Blaze. That's just her way."

Blaze waved her off. "Aw, I ain't tripping. You're welcome to have as much as you want, too, Princess. Just save some room for dessert."

"Dessert?" Screw said with a mouth full of greens. "I wonder what you done made for that?"

Flip elbowed him. "Damn, fool, close yo mouth when you eatin'. That look disgusting as hell."

Screw elbowed him back. "Yeah, well why don't you just close yo eyes when I'm talking. I likes to conversate while I eat, and I hate when somebody try and stop me."

Princess grabbed the bottle of Tabasco sauce and took off the top with food all over her hands. She had a tough time getting it off, but when she did, she grabbed another piece of chicken out of the basket and drenched it in the sauce before ripping the skin off and throwing it into her mouth, chewing with her eyes closed.

Blaze looked at her, and flared her nose. She must've felt me looking her way because we made eye contact and she winked at me.

After dinner, me and Flip stepped on the back porch, where he handed me a blunt so fat it looked like a mini sub. I put fire to it, and inhaled deeply, feeling the sting of it. It smelled and tasted even better.

"You fuck wit that Lean, homeboy?" He tried to hand me a pink Sprite.

I shook my head. "Nall, I don't like bein' all sleepy and shit. I got too much goin' on to be in a slumber. I appreciate you though."

"A'ight, so let's talk some business. My cousin got ten apartment buildings in Clover City, which is my land, that she wanna give to you for you to do your thing. I say we come up wit a scenario so all parties be able to eat good."

I don't know what kind of *loud* that was, but I was high as a muthafucka. He looked like he was in a movie, and suddenly, it got humid as hell. "Yo, so what do you propose?" I asked leaning against the banister with my eyes low.

"Tywain told me that y'all in knee deep with that Hood Rich outta Chicago. That's homie with the Rebirth, right?" He turned the Sprite up and drank a quarter of the bottle before I handed him the blunt.

"Yeah, that's big Homie. We got some major moves that we make wit him and Meech that got us eating."

Flip nodded his head hard. "I want that Rebirth out here in Clover City, man. Muhfuckas bought an ounce of that shit out here last month, and the feens ain't been right since. It's to the point that they don't even wanna buy our dope no more, and I make sure I never step on my product. It's the purest I can get.

I don't believe in fucking people over. It don't matter if they feens or not. I try and make sure they get the best deal for they paper. That's why muhfuckas drivin' all the way to Houston to fuck wit me. I want that Rebirth, homeboy, and in exchange, I'll make you the mayor of my city in this underworld. We tried to reach out to Hood Rich a few years ago and he snubbed us. Can you get us in?"

I nodded. "Me and that nigga Hood Rich do good business, but I can't speak for him. I don't know if it's a reason he ain't fucking wit Texas. What I can tell you is that I'mma drop this bug in his ear, and do all I can to make this happen. I need that security in this city, and I'd appreciate it if we could fall under the same umbrella."

He smiled and rubbed his chin. "One hand washes the other, my nigga. You do your part and I'll do mine."

***

Blaze came and knocked on the guest room door where Princess and I were staying at about three in the morning. Luckily, I was up and Princess was out like a light. She had slowly opened the door and waved for me to meet her in the hallway.

I climbed out of the bed, after kissing Princess on the forehead. As soon as I got into the hallway, Blaze crashed into me, and stuck her hand down my boxers, squeezing my dick.

"I need this pipe, Taurus. I need you to fuck me real hard, so come on." She grabbed my hand and led me to her bedroom, pushing me on the bed, before jumping on top of me and pulling my boxers down. As soon as my dick sprung up, she stroked it, and slid him into her mouth, sliding all the way down until her lips were on my balls, then slurping back up to the top of him. “Ain’t nothing like sucking a big penis. Damn, you taste good.”

Chapter 11

Blaze rubbed my dick all over her face before slurping it back into her mouth just as Princess opened the door to the room and stretched out her arms into the air.

"Yeah, got me a good night's rest, now we about to explain to you why I'm his number one everything."

Blaze's eyes got as big as paper plates. She started to get off me when Princess grabbed her by the hair, and threw her on to the bed, jumping on top of her.

"I'm sorry. I didn't know. I thought-"

Princess wrapped her hand around Blaze's neck, and kissed her on the lips, sucking them loudly, before licking all over them.

"Damn, my nigga dick taste good coming off yo lips." She bit into her neck and Blaze moaned.

I slid my hand into Blaze's panties and rubbed all over her naked pussy lips. She was soaking wet. Her juices oozed out of her at a rapid pace. I spread her lips with two of my fingers and slid my middle one up her box.

Princess ripped her panties all the way off and threw them over her shoulder. "I wanna see what all the hype is about wit you, Blaze. My nigga just keep runnin' back to this pussy so it gotta be good." She leaned down and sucked half of her pussy lip into her mouth while my fingers drove in and out of her.

"Unnn. Unnn, awww shit," she moaned, opening her legs so wide it looked like she was trying to hit the splits.

I stuffed three fingers in her and started finger fucking her super-fast while Princess slurped and ran her tongue across her clitoris.

Blaze got to shaking and screaming at the top of her lungs. That made me speed up the pace. Then I pinched her clitoris and ran my thumb across it. All the while, Princess was flicking it with her tongue, making noises that drove me absolutely crazy.

"Yo, this bitch got me hot, daddy. I gotta rub my pussy against hers. I gotta come on this bitch." She jumped on top of her and pulled up her skirt. Wrapping one of her legs outside of Blaze's, they scissored, and Princess started pumping her hips real fast while stroking my dick up and down.

I couldn't take my eyes away from their pussies. The way they were smashing into each other's looked so damn good. Every time Princess would hump forward, her kitten lips would mash against Blaze's, and then their juices would stick to each other's lips before the ooze broke and smeared itself against both set of lips.

Blaze grabbed Princess by the ass and started fucking into her at full speed with her eyes closed. "Yes. Yes. Yes. Please, Princess. Aww shit, yes," she screamed.

I was licking all over Princess' back, and in between her ass crack. I sucked my middle finger, and slid it up her back door while reaching and grabbing a handful of Blaze's titty, pulling on the nipple harshly.

"Unnn, Unnn. Shit, daddy, you finna make your baby girl come. I'm coming daddy. I'm coming all over this pretty bitch," she moaned, closing her eyes, and pumping her hips so fast that my finger slipped out of her ass for a second. I replaced it with two and timed her movements so that we were flowing.

As soon as I felt her coming, I allowed her to shake for about ten seconds before I pushed her on top of Blaze, slid my dick in her pussy from the back, and began fucking her so hard that the headboard started slamming against the wall, knocking a picture that hung over the bed off the wall. It landed on my back and I shook it off me.

"Yes, daddy. Yes, daddy. Fuck me harder. Harder, dadddeee!"

I could see the tears rolling down her cheeks when she turned her head to the side. I kept working that ass, and she kept on slamming back into me. After I came deep within her belly, she rolled off Blaze, and I pushed Blaze's knees to her chest.

Princess laid with her head sideways on the mattress, eating Blaze for all she was worth, while she moaned at the top of her lungs. She pulled down Princess' tank top, exposing her pretty titties with the big nipples. I watched her pulling them and rubbing her thumb back and forth across them. Princess spread Blaze's lips, exposing her pink hole. "Daddy, I want you to treat this bitch. I want you to fuck her so hard that she start cryin' like I just did." She sucked on Blaze's clitoris and grabbed my dick, leading me into her.

Blazed moaned and opened her legs wider.

As soon as I felt that heat, I drove into her with so much force that she took a deep breath. I hit the bottom, slid all the way out, and forced my dick into her again. Then I started beating that shit up while Princess held her pussy lips open for me.

"Kill that shit, daddy. Let this bitch know what it is." She slid her face up and they started making out. Then Princess put her titty next to Blaze's mouth and she sucked on her nipples while Princess finger fucked herself, watching my dick go in and out of Blaze.

It ended with me hitting Blaze from the back while she ate Princess's pussy. My baby girl rubbed all over my abs as I stabbed into Blaze at full speed.

***

The next night, Hood Rich hit my phone, and we met up at First Class Divas, which was a top-notch strip club in San Antonio. He said he wanted to talk business and thought that I needed a lil' VIP treatment. I told Princess what it was, and she decided to stay back in Houston to play around with Blaze some more. I figured that once they got properly acquainted, they would hit it off.

I was met in the parking lot by four of Hood Rich's men. I could tell they were heavily armed because the handles of their gun's poked through their silk shirts. I stepped out of the stretch limo that he'd sent me with a bottle of Ace of Spades in my hand. I was already high as a muthafucka because when I got in the limo, there was a bucket of Tropical Loud waiting on me. That shit was all different colors, too, yellow, red, blue, and orange. I was high as a kite, and feeling like a boss.

I stepped in the club dressed in a red and black Ferragamo fit, with the belt and shoes to match. I even had on the Ferragamo sun visor, flipped upside down and to the back. It had been a while since I'd gotten myself dressed and put together, so I was feeling good.

As soon as I got into the door good, there was a Chinese looking broad that walked past me so thick that I had to do a double take. I had never seen an Asian that strapped before, and before I could stop myself, I grabbed her hand. "Say, lil' mama, how you doing? My name Taurus, and you bad as hell."

She looked me up and down, and put her hand on her hip as if she was trying to decide whether to take me serious or not. "Excuse you?"

I laughed a lil' bit. Then I went into my pocket and pulled out two big ass knots of hundreds. Twenty bands a piece. I had so much cash on me because after we hit that nigga Juice, instead of me and Princess trying to put that shit in the bank, we were spending it little by little. "I said my name Taurus. Now what is yours?"

There was about five strippers that stood behind her, looking me up and down with their eyes bugged out of their heads. I threw one of the knots in the air and put my arm around her.

She looked as if she was about to bend over to get some of the money, but I stopped her. "What's your name, ma?" I asked, handing her half of the other knot.

"My name Lynnx, and I just transferred down here from Long Beach."

"Well I ain't never seen no Asian chick as thick as you, and I want me and my baby mother to punish yo pussy one of these days. Let us fly you out to wherever we at, all expenses paid, and all you gotta do is open them thighs. What you think about that?"

She popped back on her legs, and that drove me crazy because I loved when a female did that. I think I was just feeling some type of way because she was Asian though. I had never seen one with so much body. "That sounds good to me. Where are you from?"

"Don't worry about all that. Just give me your information and I'mma get back up wit you Ms. Lynnx."

She hugged me and licked my ear lobe. "I'm down to do whatever you and your BM want me to do. I ain't got no inhibitions, and you fine." She walked away with her panties so far in her booty that they basically disappeared.

I couldn't do nothing but shake my head. I couldn't wait to get back to Houston so I could show Princess the pics I'd taken with my phone.

Hood Rich embraced me with a half of hug. He was a big nigga just like me, maybe a few inches shorter, but the same amount of muscle. He was dressed in a Dolce and Gabanna fit, black and yellow, with some Timbs that were unlaced. Around his neck was a big ass gold crown with diamonds. "What it do, lil' bruh? I ain't seen you in a minute."

Hood Rich was a street legend back in Chicago where I was originally from. He was from the gutta like me. He started out in the slums of the projects. When he got a little older, he found a way to capitalize off the slums. He shut down the whole city, and went on a rampage with his murderous crew. They ran into people's homes and forced them to inject The Rebirth into their veins. The Rebirth was a highly addictive chemically enhanced heroin that left dope addicts feeling like they were getting high for the first time every time. Hood Rich had gone from starving to filthy rich, in a matter of years. He was a street legend.

"Yeah, I been all over the place, trying to figure life out. You know how shit go." He handed me a fat Cuban cigar stuffed with that Tropical shit. As soon as I lit it, I could tell what it was.

His men were gathered around us, about twenty deep. They looked like pure killers with tattoos all over their faces.

Some of them were so big that you could tell that they were body builders, or either they'd just gotten out of the joint.

"Where that fool Meech at?" I asked, handing him back the blunt.

He pushed my hand away, respectfully, and held up his own stuffed Cuban. "He away, takin' care of somethin' in England that gotta be handled. I'll try and make sure he wit me the next time we meet up." He sparked the blunt, and inhaled deeply. "You know I think my right-hand man fuckin' with that Rebirth."

That caught me off guard. I watched him lean back on the couch. He dumped the ashes from his cigar into an ashtray. I did the same trying to buy time because I ain't know how to go on with the conversation.

"The worst thing that could happen to one of us, Taurus, is to start fucking wit that Rebirth. Ain't no coming back from that shit. I might have just lost my best friend."

I shook my head. "That's fucked up. Look, the reason why I reached out to you is because I wanna move out this way. I'm thinking Clover City. I got a few connects in place with a lot of property, and we wanna turn them into Rebirth depots. What you think about that?"

Hood Rich put his hand in the air and gave some sort of signal, and about ten strippers stepped past the velvet ropes and into the V.I.P. room that we were in. They were fine, too, with thick ass bodies that made me wish Princess was there.

The music started. "Bounce that ass, bounce that ass. You hoes bounce that ass." They started cutting up, shaking them fat booties.

One stripper, a brown skinned cutie that was so thick she was almost chubby, came in front of me, bent all the way over, and slid her panties down her thighs. When her pussy came into view, it was busted all the way open to the point that I could see pink. She swayed her ass from left to right, and then made her cheeks clap. I was mesmerized. Another Puerto Rican broad sat on my lap, and got to winding in slow motion. Her booty gripped my dick and rode it slowly, while she pulled her bra off and exposed her brown titties with pierced nipples.

"Yo, Taurus, why would a muthafucka need to fuck wit that Rebirth when they could be doin' this all day long?" He threw a broad off his lap, and she hit the splits on the floor, bouncing up and down. He smacked her on the ass, as two other strippers climbed on to his lap. "I'm gone fuck wit you out here, Taurus. If you think that you can take over Clover City using my product, then I'm gone support you one hundred percent. You got my blessing." He started making out with one of the Spanish chicks. "Yo, but when I need a favor from you, I don't want you to deny me. Deal?"

I leaned over and shook his hand.

***

We stayed down there for a full week before the first shipment arrived. Two hundred kilos of pure Rebirth. That nigga Flip couldn't contain himself.

"Mane, Taurus, you the shit, mane. This about to have all of us rich as a muthfucka, mane. I don't even know what to say, I owe you, homeboy."

"Just handle your business and keep your word, that's all I ask."

And we began to flood Clover City. Blaze had ten apartment buildings that were in the heart of the slums. I mean, drug *infested.* Flip and Screw set up their crews right in six of the buildings, and put the word out about the Rebirth. In less than two days, there were lines around each of the buildings that we popped the Rebirth from. I liked how them Texas niggas got down because they were all about their paper.

***

The next Saturday came, and me and Princess wound up in Chicago at the Orlando Square with a handful of shopping bags. My mother, Mary, Felicia, and Mercedes were going crazy, running in and out of the stores. Me and Princess played shit real cool like. We let them get whatever they wanted to get.

"Man, are you sure you don't want me to hit you at all for this, Taurus?" Felicia asked as the cashier rang up her four thousand five-hundred-dollar bill at Sak's Fifth Ave. She looked like she was uncomfortable.

"I shook my head. It's like I told you before, as long as you make sure my people straight, I got you. I'm gon' pay up all of your bills, too, before we leave. You need a new whip or somethin'?"

Mercedes bumped me. "I do. I been tryna get my mother to lease me one ever since I got home but she actin' like she can't hear me, and it's so annoyin'." At saying this, she rolled her eyes.

"It ain't got nothing to do with me not being able to hear you. It's all about me not being able to afford your high-priced ass. You don't want some regular starter car. You gotta have a Mercedes." Now she rolled her eyes.

"Okay, then why did you name me that then? Because it will look awfully stupid of me to be rollin' around in a Honda, but my name is Mercedes. That just don't seem right to me."

Felicia shook her head. "You see what I'm dealin' with here, don't you?"

I laughed. "If she want a Mercedes, we gon' get her one. I think she deserve it after all she went through. I got her."

Felicia dropped her bag of new clothes. "Say what?" She bent over and started picking them back up and putting them in her bag. "I know you ain't just say what I think you did, did you?"

I laughed. "Yeah, I got her. I mean, she done been kid-napped and screwed over by that nigga Monty. The least I can do is put her in a new whip."

"Shid, then what about me. It sho' ain't gon' look right wit my daughter drivin' a new Mercedes, and there I am in my old ass Buick. Where they do that at?"

Princess walked over holding Jahliya and put her arms around my neck. "Yo, you hoez better back up off my man. If anybody gon' be gold diggin' him, it's gonna be me. Y'all ain't givin' up no pussy, and you ain't had his child, so step the fuck back." She curled her upper lip and looked from one of them to the other.

I didn't know if she was serious or not because the tone in her voice was iffy. She handed Jahliya to me, and I got to kiss-ing all over her chubby cheeks while she laughed and laughed.

"You ain't gotta come at us like that," Felicia said, frown-ing.

"Yeah, that was rude as hell," Mercedes agreed, standing behind her mother.

Princess rolled her head around on her shoulders. "Y'all ain't gotta be all over him like that, tryin' to hit his pockets. It ain't sweet. I know y'all kin, but that only go so far. He still my man, at the of the day, and I run this." She cuffed my dick in her hand.

I pushed her hand away as the white lady behind the counter gave me a look that said she was ready to call security. That was all that me and Princess needed.

Felicia stepped into her face. "You lucky he is my cousin, because if he wasn't, I'd fuck him so good that he'd forget about yo ass. You might be bad, bitch, but you ain't got all of this right here." She cuffed her own ass, and jiggled the cheeks.

I was glad when my mother walked over. "Look, y'all, stop acting like y'all ain't got no good sense. And, Felicia, let yo ass go. Everybody know you got a little booty, big freaking deal. I do, too, but I don't go around cupping it in people's faces."

Princess was mugging the shit out of Felicia at that time.

"You should, mama, at least yours look right on you. She popped to me, and her body ain't all that."

"Excuse you," Mercedes said, stepping from behind Felicia. "Must you insist on being so rude to my mother?"

"Lil' girl, go find you a hobby," Princess said, bumping them out of the way, and leaving the store.

I handed my daughter to my mother. "Hold on, mama, let me see what's wrong wit her." I jogged behind her to catch up, and met up with her as she was going into the bathroom.

I opened the door behind her, stepped in, and saw her pacing back and forth. The bathroom was luckily empty. "I don't like them bitches. Them hoes wanna fuck you, and its pissing me off. I just wish I could have you all to myself, and share you wit a bitch every now and then. I don't like yo family 'cuz it seem like all the hoes in it wanna give you they pussy."

I felt like she was overreacting, but I was smart enough to know not to poke the bear of her attitude when she was mad. I didn't think that Felicia or Mercedes looked at me like that, and if they did, I wasn't going. I had that forbidden shit in me, but it wasn't so bad that I was trying to smash every female of my bloodline.

"Yo, so what you want me to do, baby, because I can't have you feeling some type of way all day long. I wanna thank them for keeping our people safe, and buying them a whip a piece ain't gone hurt us. We got three hundred fifty thousand in cash to play wit, and all type of paper in the bank. Why we can't splurge a lil' bit?"

A fat chick came into the bathroom, so big that she looked like she ate two second graders. She was pulling her pants down and searching for an empty stall. I could hear her farting all loud and everything. She had the nerves to have a Chipotle bag in her hand that looked like it was filled to the max. When she saw me, she froze in place, and farted again. "Uh, you can't be in here, this is the women's bathroom."

Princess pinched her nose. "You stanky ass bitch, he know what bathroom he in. Mind yo fucking business for I kick the shit out you, literally." Princess balled up her fists, and eyed the woman with obvious anger.

The fat chick farted again, and stepped into a stall, closing the door and locking it. "Oooh shit. Un. I was just-. Oh shit. Sayin' that he can't be in here."

I heard one of her turds splash into the water, and then it started to smell like the strongest version of shit that I had ever smelled, and Jahliya did damage in her pampers.

"Damn, bitch, you stank," Princess yelled. She kept pinching her nose, and I followed her out of the bathroom.

We wound up in the car with the radio banging that Yo Gotti. "Like I said, I just don't like the way they be looking at you. Them bitches be jockin' you like you they last meal. Word is bond. I caught both of them lustin' more than once. I think the daughter wanna fuck you more than her mother do." She shook her head, reached under the seat, and came up with a .45. She cocked it back. "I feel like killing something. When was the last time we smoked somebody?"

I looked up and saw my mother, sister, daughter and cousins making their way to the car. They couldn't have been more than a football field away. "Yo, Princess, put that burner back under the seat, and chill the fuck out. Right now, we gotta lay low for a minute. Let's spend some time with our daughter, and then we can figure everything else out. But for right now, I'mma need you to chill. "

She flared her nose. "A'ight, daddy, I hope I can leave Chicago without bustin' one of they ass. I ain't playin' about you, just like you ain't playin' about me. This shit that we got goin' ain't no game." She slid the burner back under the seat, and put a phoney ass smile on her face. "Better?"

***

"Oooh, Taurus, let me get that purple one right there," Mercedes said, pointing to a Mercedes AMG "I promise, when I get my bands up, I'll pay you back," she said, putting her hands together like she was praying.

Princess rolled her eyes. “First, you gotta get a job, then we can start to believe that you gone try and pay us back.”

“Damn, what is your problem, cousin?” Mercedes asked Princess, while walking over to my mother.

Princess shrugged her shoulders. “I’m PMSin’ right now and everything irritatin’ me.” She curled her lip.

I put my arm around her shoulder and whispered in her ear. “Baby, that just mean we gotta get a lil’ gross tonight. You need daddy to beat that bloody shit in and I got you. Just chill. Let’s take care of them, so we can get back to the basics.”

She giggled. “Okay, daddy.”

I copped Mercedes the whip she wanted, and Felicia the Benz Truck. I asked my mother if she wanted to ride foreign, too, but she asked for the cash, so I wound up giving her a cool fifty gees.

After my mother took care of the paperwork, we all went out to a steak house and had a nice meal. I had to fuck Princess in the bathroom because she kept getting into it with both of my cousins. I noted while I was rocking her ass that her period had come down, so I chopped her attitude up to that.

That night, out of all the places I could have wound up, I found myself in church, bent down on my knees with Princess right beside me. It was strictly an impulse thing. I didn’t plan it, we just wound up there.

Princess inhaled a deep breath and blew it out. “So, what do we do now?”

“We pray, baby. You can tell Jehovah anything that you wanna tell Him and He gon’ listen to you.”

"Well, I don't really know what to say because we been doin' a lot of shi-, I mean, stuff. What if He get mad because I'm trying to talk to Him?"

I tried to get a little more comfortable on my knees. "Baby, it don't go like that. He'll never get mad at you for tryin' to holler at Him."

"He will once He remember how many people we killed." She gave me a look like she was scared.

"Look, Princess, He already knew you was going to be a killer before you bodied your first person. He's the Creator of all things. It's just like a person that writes a book. They pretty much know what they want their characters to be like before they type the first line of that character. So how we get down ain't no surprise to Him?"

"So, you mean to tell me that he knew we was gon' kill that white lady and man at the lakefront?"

I shrugged my shoulders. "Yep, he know everything you gone do before you do it, I guess."

"Dang, that sound scary. That mean we ain't nothing but toys to Him then." She looked like she wanted to stand up.

"Baby, where are you goin'?" I asked, getting a little irritated.

"It don't make no sense to pray if He already know what I'm gon' say, and what I've already done. That would be so annoying if a person started telling me everything that I already knew. I done did enough wrong. I ain't trying to piss him off even more."

I smiled, even though my heart was beating fast. I knew that she was just naive and didn't know how the God thing worked. But I was a believer in the Lord above, and I honestly knew that me and Princess was going to be together until He took me off the face of this Earth, so I wanted to pray over us, and our union. "Okay, baby, well can you at least allow me to pray to Him for us?"

"Okay, I can do that, but if He get mad at us because of you wanting to get His attention all of the sudden, I'm gone be kicking yo tail the whole time we down there in hell." I could tell that she wasn't joking.

"Man, close yo eyes," I said, putting her hands within mine. I took a deep breath, and exhaled. "Father, in the might name of Jesus, me and my woman come to You humbly and submissively, asking that You receive our prayers and praise. Jehovah, we know that we've been out here doing a bunch of wrong. We've been killing, and doing every sin under the sun. But I ask, in the mighty name of Jesus, that You forgive us of our sins, and for all of those that we have trespassed against. Please protect our daughter, and the rest of our family. Please don't allow for them to be punished on our behalf. Forgive us of our sins, Father, as You know that we are nowhere near done. But I ask that you wash us clean, this day, and that You strengthen us in the days to come. For we know that no weapons formed against us shall prosper, and that You are our Father and ultimate protection. In Jesus' holy and precious name we pray. Amen."

"Amen," Princess said, opening one eye and looking up at the sky with it like Jehovah was about to strike us down with lightning.

I got up and sat on the wooden bench. "How do you feel, baby?" I helped her up and sat her next to me, kissing her cheek.

"I don't know. I think I feel the same. Why, how am I supposed to feel?"

"I don't know, baby."

Chapter 12

Princess woke me out of my sleep early the next morning by pushing me in the chest. “Baby, it’s Blaze on the phone. She sayin’ that Tywain got stabbed two hundred times in that jail, and that he dead!” she yelled.

I shot up and grabbed the phone from her. “Hello.”

“My cousin dead, Taurus. They found him in the shower with over two hundred stab wounds. They waiting to do a full autopsy report, but they’re already saying that it was the cause of death.”

“Do they know who did it?” I asked, feeling the tears roll down my cheeks.

“I don’t know. They ain’t said nothing about it to me yet, and I’m his emergency contact. I’m devastated. I don’t know what to do.”

“The only thing we can do is bury him like a G, until we can figure out what happened. Me and you gone take care of this together. I got you.”

“I appreciate that. Make sure you send my love to Princess and let her know to call me later on tonight. I gotta get my head together.”

As soon as I hung up the phone, I dropped to my knees, crying like a baby. Tywain was my nigga, and I ain’t never loved no man as much as I loved him. Since the first day that we met, we’d been as thick as thieves, and down for each other. I committed my first murder with him, and I was gone take his death hard.

Princess knelt down from the bed and wrapped her arms over me. She was crying just as hard. I felt her shivering, and that made me feel some type of way. “I love you, daddy, and

I don't like seeing you break down like this. I'm right here if you need a shoulder to lean on. I'll do anything to make you feel better."

I turned all the way around and pulled her into my arms. I squeezed her tightly and kissed the tears that were on her cheeks. "Baby, that was my nigga. I been through everything wit him. That nigga saved my life on many occasions, and I did the same for him." I pulled her to me even more. "Do you have any idea how hard it is to find a stomp down homie that never crosses you? The homie ain't never crossed me. He been more of a brother to me than my own blood." I just had to let them waterworks go. I couldn't hold that shit in no more.

Princess rubbed my back. "I love you so much, daddy. Please get this out of you. I don't like seeing you like this. If you cry, then that means that we're in trouble. It means that we're too weak to fight on, so you scarin' me right now." She started to shake even harder.

As I felt that, I snapped out of it. She was right. I couldn't be there in that moment, losing myself. I mean, it was true that Tywain was my heart, and I was gone miss him. But I had a more important task of protecting my baby girl. When she saw me weak, she felt ten times weaker, so it was my job to control my emotions, and to conquer myself. I took a deep breath and stood all the way up.

She stood and wiped my tears away. "Are you okay now, daddy? What can I do to make you feel better?"

Before I could answer her, my phone vibrated. That nigga Juice's picture popped up. Princess grabbed it and put him on speakerphone. He started out by laughing. "Ding dong, that bitch ass nigga is dead. Blood in Blood out. They said he hollered like a bitch getting raped when that metal was going in and out of his ass. I guess he wasn't so tough after all, huh?"

"You know what, Juice, you ain't nothin' but a muthafuckin' coward! You don't put in no work for yourself. When was the last time you kilt a nigga on yo own?"

"When I cut yo aunty into a hundred pieces." He started laughing so loud that it echoed in our hotel room. Princess picked up the phone ready to throw it against the wall, but I stopped her.

I grabbed the phone out of her hand. "Juice, let's settle this shit once and for all. Nigga, I'll meet you anywhere. You pick the time and the place, and I'll be there. No guns, we can fight to the death like men. Or we can play wit them hammers. However you wanna do it."

"Who is that, Taurus, talking all gangsta and shit?" He started laughing again. "Nigga, shut yo bitch ass up. You ain't 'bout that life. That lil' bitch got you thinking that you a rider now, huh? What, because y'all kilt Mardi? It didn't take no balls to do that."

"It didn't take no balls for you to kill my aunty either. Nigga, you ain't as hard as you front to be. You probably so damn evil cause yo dick so small. That ain't the world's fault."

Now he was really laughing like a fool. "Yo, on my Blood, whenever I see either one of you bitches, I'm knocking yo head off. If I find where our mother at, I'm knocking her head off. Mary, her head coming off. Y'all daughter, I'm cutting that lil' bitch head off, too. That's my word. Nigga, this is war. We gone see who survive." The phone went dead.

"I hate that nigga," Princess said, swinging at the air.

***

Blaze said that Tywain had always wanted to be buried in his homeland of Brooklyn, New York. It took us ten days to take care of all of the arrangements, but when it was all said and done, we wound up throwing him a beautiful ceremony at Ebenezer Baptist Church. It was the same church where he had been baptized when he was only ten years old.

I couldn't even look down at the homie when I walked past his casket at first. It took all of the man in me to keep from breaking down. We'd dressed him up in a black and red Burberry tux with the bow tie. They had to put a net over his face because he'd been stabbed seventy-five times in it, and the bitch niggas that did it had pulled out both of his eyes in the process.

Princess came up behind me in her all black Prada dress and rubbed my back. "It's gone be okay, baby. We gone get that nigga Juice, you better believe that."

"I know, ma. I just hate seeing my nigga in this condition. I guarantee this gone be the last real nigga I ever have in my life." I shook my head and looked down at him thoroughly for the first time. I placed my hand on his chest. "I love you, nigga. And I'm gone avenge your death. Word is bond."

Princess came up to his casket and laid her hand on his chest as well. "We'll see you later, homie. It probably won't be long."

After that, the choir got up and sang a selection. I wrapped my arm around Princess and held my daughter as she slept. My mother took her out of my arms. "Come on and let me hold her. She gone get a crook in her neck."

After the choir sang, the preacher, some older heavy-set man, got up, grabbed the microphone, and cleared his throat.

But before he could get any words out, the doors to the church flew open, and what seemed like fifteen niggas ran in with assault rifles in their hands. They aimed at Tywain's casket and let loose.

Brrrr bocka! Brrr bocka! Brrr bocka! Boom! Boom! Boom!

The bullets tore into Tywain's casket and knocked it over. He rolled out of it and on to his face.

I pushed my mother and sister to the ground. "Y'all stay down here and don't move." I slowly stood, and peeked over the wooden bench that we were sitting in. Pulling out my .40 caliber, I cocked it, and aimed at the shooter closest to us.

Boo-ah. Boo-ah. Boo-ah.

The bullet caught him in the neck and he fell backward, holding it with blood seeping through his fingers.

Princess crawled on the floor with her .9 millimeter, aimed at one of the shooters, and pulled the trigger.

Bocka. Bocka.

He fell after taking two to the back. Now the attention was turned our way.

Brrr bocka. Brrr bocka. Brrr bocka. Boom. Boom. Boom.

Big chunks of wood were knocked out of the benches. I heard somebody scream, and I looked to make sure that it wasn't my mother or sister. There were big clouds of gun smoke in the air. I aimed my gun over the top of the seat and busted twice.

Boo-ah! Boo-ah! I didn't know who I was aiming at, I just wanted to let them niggas know that we was strapped. I heard the door open and looked to see all the shooters running out, except for the two that laid dead in the middle of the church.

So, as they retreated, me and Princess decided to chase them busting back to back.

Bocka. Bocka. Boo-ah. Boo-ah.

They jumped into a black Excursion and peeled away from the curb, fish tailing. I busted, aiming at their back window.

Boo-ah.

It shattered and the truck swerved and smacked a parked car before storming down the street in the other direction.

"What type of niggas shoot up a funeral? Seem like niggas getting more and more bitch like these days," I said, following Princess back into the church.

Inside, it was chaos. Little kids were crying and hugging on to the pant legs of their parents. The pastor was kneeling beside one of the dead shooters saying some type of prayer over him.

I looked around for my mother and family, and saw that they were at the front of the church, trying to roll Tywain back inside of his casket. I jogged down the aisle. My sister ran into my arms before I could get to the front to help my mother and some other people get my right-hand man back into his coffin.

"Taurus, I'm scared. I want you to get us out of here before those men come back and kill us," Mary whimpered, holding on to me tightly.

I hugged her and kissed her forehead. "Alright, boo, just let me help them get him up."

She nodded and reluctantly let me go. "I'm gone grab our coats, then let's leave, please."

"Alright, boo."

Princess came over and we helped my mother and some other people get Tywain back into his coffin. There were dents in the side of it were the bullets had slammed into the exterior.

The net had come off his face and, for the first time, I was able to see the damage that the prisoners had done to him. His face looked like a pin cushion. I felt myself getting emotionally weak, thinking about them niggas jumping and taking advantage of him. I wished I would have been there. I would have fought with my homie until the death.

"Yo, let's get out of here, Taurus. Ain't no sense in trying to bury him, you already know the police about to be all over this muh-"

Boom! The explosion was so loud that I went deaf for a minute. On instinct, I grabbed Princess and pulled her to the floor, throwing my body on top of hers. "Stay yo ass down!"

I didn't know what was going on, and then I heard something being smashed or rolled over. People started to scream, and it felt like the ground was vibrating.

"Taurus! Help me," I heard my little sister scream.

I guessed that I had closed my eyes because when I opened them, I turned to see the whole front of the church had been crashed through by a big ass black Hummer. Five men jumped out of it with red bandanas across their faces. The sixth man that stepped out was Juice, and he had a big ass assault rifle in his hands. He snatched my sister by her hair and threw her in the truck. Then he aimed at me and Princess.

Thaaat-dat! Thaaat-da! Thaaat-dat!

The bullets slammed into Tywain's coffin. I pulled Princess up and we dove behind it, returning fire.

Boo-ah! Boo-ah! Boo-ah! Bocka! Bocka! Bocka!

But once his men started firing at us, it was too much, especially since I was out of bullets, and after her last shot, she was, too. I grabbed her by the hand and pulled her to the stairway, which we hid behind.

"Aw shit, Jahliya," Princess screamed, and was about to run back out into the gunfire.

I yanked her back to me as the bullets slammed into the wall right by us and a chunk of dry wall exploded into our faces. I started coughing and so did she.

"Look, I'm out of bullets. If we go back out there, Juice gon' kill us. Then we ain't gon' be able to protect Jahliya at all. We gotta be smart." I mean, it killed me to speak that wisdom to her because I wanted to save our daughter. It made me feel less of a man in that moment. But I had to be smart.

Juice got behind the wheel and stepped on the gas, crashing into Tywain's coffin, and rolling over it. He must've spotted my mother crouching down because he pointed at her and two of his men ran and snatched her up by her hair. She had Jahliya in her arms.

"An eye for an eye, bitch nigga. Get in, bitch, before I blow yo head off," he said, grabbing my mother by the throat and slinging her into the back of the Hummer. "Aye, Taurus, I'mma fuck this bitch, too, just like you did. Every nigga wanna see what they mama shit like anyway. Well I'mma find out for myself. Then I'mma kill her and Mary."

He jumped back in the Hummer and waited for his Blood niggas to get in before he backed it out of the church with me chasing it. He got all the way outside before they got to busting at me. *Thaaaat-Booyah!*

I dove on to the grass and hid behind the big church welcoming sign. When they pulled off down the street, I ran back into the church and found Princess in the middle of the aisle with her gun to her head, steady pulling on the trigger. Luckily it was empty.

Chapter 13

"He fucked us again, Taurus. He fucked us again. How do this shit keep happenin'?" Princess hollered as I sped down the alley behind the church.

There were all kinds of sirens off in the distance, but getting closer. We had to get the fuck out of there or risk being hauled in for questioning, followed by a numerous amount of charges.

"Baby, I don't know. We all the way out in New York. Who would have thought that nigga would show up all the way out here?" I slammed my hands on the steering wheel again and again.

"Fuck! And now he got our daughter, Taurus! You know he finna kill her like we killed his." Her voice started to break up as if she was about to cry. "I can't take this shit no more. It's just way too much."

I swerved out of the alley and hit the intersection, making a strong right and hopping on the expressway. Once I got on it, I felt like we were in the clear. "Baby, I don't know how we gone figure it out, but we are. We gone get our daughter back, her and my mother and sister. I ain't giving up just yet." I was trying so desperately to believe in the words that I was spitting, but the truth was that I had very little faith in them. A part of me felt like he was going to kill all of them, or at least one. It didn't take long for that theory to come into fruition.

***

It had only been three days since Tywain's funeral when Juice hit my phone at three in the morning. I was snuggled in the bed with Princess, after holding her all night while she cried and cried over our daughter. So, when the phone vibrated, I had just fallen asleep.

"Taurus, wake yo bitch ass up and come save our sister. Oops, my bad, it's too late for all of that. Go look in yo car, nigga, and be thankful that I ain't wet you and that bitch up yet. I'm havin' too much fun right now." The phone went dead.

I jumped out of the bed and threw my Jordans on. I didn't even take the time to get dressed. All I had on was my boxers and shoes. I grabbed my .40 Glock from under my pillow and made a beeline for the door, neglecting to take the elevator in the hotel. I jumped down the stairs four at a time, until I was in the parking lot. It was raining so hard outside that I was drenched as soon as I stepped out into it. I ran to my car.

When I got there, I saw that the back window was busted out on the right side. I turned around and scanned the area, holding the gun up, trying to locate anything or anyone that seemed as if they were a threat. Thunder boomed overhead, and the lightning flashed across the sky, illuminating it. I took a few steps forward and peered through the back broken window. What I saw, made me want to throw up. There was my sister, Mary's body in the back seat with a seat belt across her torso, but she was headless. There was a bunch of blood pouring out of where her neck should have been, and it smelled horrible. I opened the door, and stuck my head in, looking around to see what all was left of her. Everything was intact except for her neck and head.

I damn near shit on myself when Princess laid her hand on my back. I jumped up and bumped my head on the top of the roof inside of the car. "Baby, what's the matter? Why are you out here right now?" she asked with the rain beating on her face.

"Mary dead, baby. This nigga cut her head off. That's her body right there," I said, pointing to the back seat.

Princess stuck her head in the car. "Holy shit! Why would he do that to her? What have she ever done to him?" she asked, shaking her head.

"Nothin', that nigga just sick in the head." I didn't know whether to take my sister out of the car or leave her in there. I didn't think we could have given her much of a funeral. And we couldn't call the police because me and Princess were still wanted in Tennessee. So, I was stuck between a rock and a hard place.

"Daddy, what do we do?" she asked as the lightning struck about twenty yards away from us.

Voom! Chissssssh!.

A car window shattered and Princess looked like she was ready to run. "Ain't much we really can do right now because she gone, baby. We can't leave her in this car, though, because we been all in it. Our fingerprints are everywhere."

Just then, three squad cars appeared, seemingly out of the blue and flashed their lights. "Fuck, daddy, that's the police. Get in the car," Princess said. She knelt down and fired three shots.

Bocka! Bocka! Bocka!

I jumped into the driver's seat, started the engine, and pulled off in the car, zig-zagging. I gunned the engine headed straight for one of the police cars. It was the only exit and I was taking it. I prayed that he drove away, but the driver was cocky. He didn't seem like he was going to move, and I didn't have the time to maneuver, so I slammed into his patrol car, smashing his front end, and knocking his car to the side. The airbags deployed in our whip, and the collision caused my sister's body to be thrown into the front with us.

Princess laid still with her head against the airbag.

"Baby. are you okay? Baby, wake up," I hollered, trying to get my sister's body out of the divider in between us. It was heavy and leaking blood everywhere. I turned right and side swiped another police car before stepping on the gas and storming down the side street, and then taking an alley. I must have done a hundred miles an hour before bringing the car to a halt once that alley ended. Then I stepped on the gas after looking both ways, entering another alley and pushing the car to its limit.

Scuurrreee!

My tires screamed as I made a left, taking a side street, then hitting another alley and nearly hitting a bum who was jogging down it with some newspaper over his head. I looked into my rearview mirror and didn't see any police lights, so I made another right, and then a left, pulling up into the first open garage that I saw. As soon as I was parked, I threw open my door, and ran around and pulled Princess out, throwing her over my shoulder before jogging into the backyard of the residence whose garage we were parked in. I ran around the front with her and beat on their door, and rang the doorbell.

It seemed like it must have been three hours later, but I knew that it was only about a minute before a lady answered the door in her robe. She opened it. "Yes, may I help you?" she asked, looking me up and down.

"Ma'am, I just found this woman in the alley. I think she might have been raped. Can I please use your phone?"

"Oh Lord, yes, child, please, come in." She moved to the side and turned the lights on.

I stepped into the living room with Princess still on my shoulders. I laid her on the couch in which the lady had covered in plastic anyway. "Princess, wake up, ma," I said, feeling my throat get tight. I was worried about my Baby Girl. I was praying that she'd just been knocked out by the impact and that nothing serious had taken place with her. I didn't know what I would do, but I did know that life would not be an option for me. I needed her. The truth was the truth.

A big ass dog ran up on me and started barking. It looked like it was a Boxer. It must have weighed every bit of two hundred pounds. Then another one came, about the same size, slowly making its way to me with its ears back and K-9's bared.

"Aye, lady, come get yo dogs before they kill me in here," I yelled, going in my waistband and pulling out my Glock. I was ready to shoot them dogs dead right where they growled. There was no way that I was about to let them hurt me or my baby girl.

Just as I was about to start shooting, the black lady came into the room and slapped her hands together. "Hey, get the fuck out of here, now! Y'all know better."

I watched them lower their heads and slowly back out of the room, never taking their eyes off me. I could tell that if she had never come into the room, they would have probably tried to kill me and Princess. I would have had to shoot them dead, and then the black lady.

"I'm sorry about that." She handed me a cell phone.

"Those are my protectors right there. They make sure that nothing happens to me, and they hate men. So, I'm guessing that they smell the testosterone coming from you and it makes them want to kill you. They were trained that way." She looked over at Princess. "How is she doing?"

I shrugged my shoulders. "I don't know."

The old Lady raised her eyebrow. "Where did you say you found her at again?"

I saw flashing lights go pass her window outside. First, one set, and then about four more sets. I figured that the police were circling the area. I didn't know what to do. "She was behind your house, in the alley, just lying there. I don't know if she fell out or what."

Three more sets of flashing lights rolled down her street.

She walked to the window and looked out of it. "Boy, something must of happen. They got police all over. I hope ain't nobody got killed," she said, scratching her head, and then fixing the scarf that was wrapped around it. "This is an okay neighborhood, one of the reasons I moved into it. Can't stand being around all that chaos. I'm forty-six years old. I just want to live life now. I used to be in the streets, too. Oh yeah, I wasn't always this God-fearing woman. Back in the day, I would have never just let no anybody come into my house in the middle of the night. I would have thought you was out to kill me. But I done changed. Lord knows I done changed." She started laughing out loud, hugging herself.

"What that old geezer over there talking about, daddy?" Princess said, trying to come to a sitting position on the couch.

I felt my heat skip a beat. I leaned down and started hugging her so tight that she started hitting me on the back like I was killing her. "Oh shit, my bad, baby." I pulled her up and started kissing all over her. "I love you so much, boo. I thought you wasn't gone never wake up."

The older black woman stepped over to the couch and looked down on us like we had lost our minds. "I thought you said you found her in the alley?" She started to back away, looking us over very closely.

"Okay, let me just tell you the truth. This is my woman, and somebody just robbed us a block over. They tried to kill us, but we got away."

She gave me a look that said she wasn't buying the lie that I was telling her. She backed away a little more as three more sets of flashing lights passed behind her, flying down the street.

"Look, I don't know what y'all have done, but I want you out of my house this instant. Get thee behind me, Satan. Get thee behind me, right now."

I stood up. "Aye, listen, we ain't no damn devils. We just ran into some bad luck tonight and we needed help. Here you can have this." I went into my pocket to pull out some cash when my Glock fell from my hip and hit the floor. "Shit!"

Then she backed all the way up to the window. "Get thee behind me, Satan. I ain't ready to die." She whistled so loud that it hurt my ears. I heard a pitter patter of paws on the floor, and then her big ass dogs ran back into the living room and stopped beside her, looking up for a command.

Princess stood up with her hands out in front of her. "Say, lady, you betta tell them dogs to go back where they carne from or its gon' get ugly in here. I ain't about to play with them or you. She cocked back her .44 Desert Eagle and aimed it at the lady.

"Get thee behind me, Satan. For God so loved the world that He gave His only begotten son that whosoever believe in him shall not perish, but have everlasting life. I believe in you,

Jesus. I know that no weapons formed against me shall prosper. I know that You are the Way, the Truth, and the Light. Forgive me for my sins, and don't let them demons take me out the game. Kill," she hissed.

As soon as she did, her dogs jumped into the air, headed right for me.

Boo-wa!! Princess fired, knocking meat out of the first dog's head. His brains splashed against the curtains. His body landed on its side with its paws still kicking.

The older lady started to scream. "Oh my God. You killed my dog, you bitch. You killed my fucking dog." She ran at Princess and tackled her over the sofa. They landed with a loud boom, and got to fighting for the gun like animals. The second dog grabbed me by the arm with his teeth and started to shake. *Grrrr.* It growled, twisting his head from right to left. I wrapped my other arm around its head, placing him in a headlock, and fell backward on to her hardwood floors with him. *Errpp,* he yelped, and let go of his grip. He backed all the way up with blood running out of his nose. He placed his paw over it. I could see that it was crooked. I ran at him at full speed and kicked the shit out of him. He flew backward against the window, and landed on his side. He struggled to get up for a minute, and then rushed me with blood dripping past his mouth.

I caught him, wrapped my arms around him, and slammed him to the ground on his head. Then I started to stomp him repeatedly, while he yelped and screeched.

The older lady was on top of Princess trying to choke her to death. I heard her gagging, and gasping for air. I jumped up, after snapping the dog's neck, and grabbed the woman by her hair. Her wig came right off, and she kept on choking Princess.

Princess tried to push the woman off her, but she wouldn't budge. Once again, I grabbed her by her now nappy ass fro, and slung her off my woman. She landed against the glass table. Shattering it.

Tissssh.

Princess jumped up and ran full speed at the woman, jumping in the air and corning down with both feet on her chest. "You punk ass bitch!" she hollered, getting back up and rubbing her neck.

"I saw her bend down and pick up the gun just as we heard sirens right outside of the house, followed by car doors being slammed.

"Baby, chill, don't kill her."

She lowered her eyes. "Nall, fuck that. This bitch just tried to take me out the game wit her strong ass. Here I am thinkin' I'm gon' be able to just toss her off of me, and this bitch strong as a body builder. Fuck that. I'm whackin' her ass." She aimed at the woman's head and bit into her bottom lip.

The woman started wheezing. She stood up and put her hands in the air. "Baby, please. Please. Please, don't kill me. I'm too young to die, baby. I can't even-" She put her hand over her heart and fell to her knees.

Somebody started beating on the door, and then we heard a bunch of people running up the stairs. The beating got harder and louder.

"Its New York Police Department, is anybody home?" the officer asked with a booming voice.

The older woman dropped to the floor on her back. She started to wheeze and shake slightly while Princess looked down on her with hatred in her eyes. "I don't give a fuck. Die, bitch," she said, kneeling down over her.

I started to panic and wondered if she heard the police beating on the door. "Baby, did you hear who on the porch?" She waved me off. "I don't care. I want this bitch to die or I'm about to put a bullet in her head. This hoe tried to kill me. I gotta see her die."

The banging started on the door again. "New York City Police, is there anybody home?"

"Fuck, Princess, well at least pull that bitch into the room over there."

I grabbed one of her legs and Princess grabbed the other one, and we drug her in the room, and I closed the door behind me. My heart was beating fast, and I could barely think straight. I had to make a decision fast because I knew it wouldn't be long before the police were knocking down the door. I hurried up and grabbed the dead dogs and pulled them into a closet, turning the light off in the living room. I stopped and took off all my clothes, and answered the door naked as a Jaybird.

"Who the fuck is it beatin' on my door at this time of the mornin'?" I asked as I swung open the door and was met with a tall police officer that looked like David Batista. I mean, he was huge.

He looked down on me, saw that I was naked, and shielded his eyes. "Sir, would you mind putting on some clothes?" The other officers behind him were about four deep. They turned their heads away as well.

"Yes, I would mind going' to put on some clothes because I'm getting' ready to go back to sleep once you leave me the hell alone. Now me and my wife gotta get up in two hours. Why the fuck are you beatin' on my door like you some kind of a lunatic? I pay my mortgage every month on time. Don't tell me you come tryin' to take my house away." I started digging in my nose, and when I was done, I ate the booger. I felt like throwing up afterward, but it was better than going to jail.

"Sir we found a vehicle in your garage that took part in a homicide by mutilation, and an attempted homicide on an officer. Now those are pretty serious charges. The car is parked in your garage."

"Umm hmm, well I ain't got no car, and ain't had one ever since my accident. I don't know which one of those kids parked in my garage now, but they always got a car in there. They done found more than one stolen in there before, and that ain't have nothin' to do with me, just like this don't. If I had a car, it would be parked in there, but I don't, so it ain't." I started to close the door on him. "Now I'd appreciate it if you removed that car and allowed me to get back to sleep. I got a big day tomorrow, cleanin' up the subway. I need every bit of sleep I can get, thank you kindly."

As I was closing the door, he put his foot in it to stop it. "I'm sorry, sir, but it's not that easy. You see, technically, if you are the owner of this property, you are responsible for any vehicle that is parked here. So, if you don't mind, I'd like to step in and ask you a few questions." He started to step into the house.

I blocked his path. "Well, unfortunately, I do mind, and unless you pull out a search warrant, you ain't getting up in here. I know what y'all police be doing to black men like me, killing us and all sorts of thangs. If you think you gone do any of that to me, you got another thing coming."

"Sir, I-"

"Baby, what is goin' on out here?" Princess said, putting her arm around my neck. She had on a pink robe that I imagined was the older lady's. "I'm tryin' to get some sleep. I gotta get up in less than two hours."

"Ma'am, maybe we can talk to you. You see, we found a car parked in your garage with a dead body inside of it. The car was also used to crash into a police cruiser. The officer had to be rushed to the hospital with serious injuries. Now if I could come inside and talk to you for a minute, I'm sure that we could clear all of this up."

"Oh my God, a dead body? Well we don't have no car, or anything like that, ever since the crash, but I wouldn't mind you stepping in long as we can get dressed first." She put her two hands over my dick, blocking it from their view.

"Please give us five minutes. It's all we'll need, sir."

The big wrestler looking man nodded and smiled. "That will be fine."

I stepped back in and closed the door. "What the fuck are you talking about? Ain't no way they gone be able to come in here and not figure everything out." I was panicking.

"I know that, fool. Don't you think I got a little sense up here?" she said, pointing to her brain. "Just get dressed and follow me."

As soon as I got dressed, she grabbed my hand and took me up the stairs, but not before we went through the bedroom where I saw that the older woman had passed out and died. She laid in the middle of the floor with her eyes wide open.

Princess ran up the stairs two at a time with me following behind her. When we got to the very top, she took me to a door that led out to a back balcony. She climbed out onto it.

"Okay, baby, come on."

I stepped onto it, and looked at her like she was crazy. Down below I could hear the sounds of the police officers' walkie-talkies. Their cars were lined up in front of the house with all of them on the porch, awaiting us to let them in. I watched Princess back all the way up, and then run at full speed, jumping and landing on the balcony next door. She waved for me to do the same.

My heart got to beating harder than an African drummer. I backed up to the railing, and then ran full speed ahead, jumping, and landing on the same balcony that she stood on. "Fuck," I said, hitting my knees.

But she was already up and jumping onto the next balcony. I followed close behind and did the same thing. We wound up jumping onto nine balconies before we climbed down the side of the last house and took off running full speed down the street. We crossed it and ran down that alley until we came to a gas station.

"Fuck, I can barely breathe," she said with her chest heaving up and down. She pulled up her pant leg, and I saw that she had scraped her knee real bad. It was bleeding profusely.

I looked over to the gas station and saw a car roll in with tinted windows. It was all red with gold rims and beating out of control. The Corvette was clean. It parked in front of a gas pump, and a dude got out with some real long dreads, and a lot of gold around his neck. He looked like 2 Chainz.

"Yo, boo, you see that nigga right there?" I asked cocking my Glock.

She licked her lips and squinted her eyes. "Yeah, I see him. He about to become prey, huh?"

I smiled. "You already know." I crouched down low to the ground and came from the side of the gas station. By the time he saw me, it was too late. Princess was jumping in his car, and I raised the gun and pointed it at him. "Look, bro, don't make me splash you. Just walk over here real cool like, and you can keep yo blood inside of your body. All we want is the whip."

He looked both ways, like he wanted to see who all was witnessing him being robbed. "Yo, you can have my car, homie, it ain't no big deal. But I ain't about to follow you in no alley, that's suicide." He started to walk closer to the gas station's entrance.

"Look, nigga, if you think I'm playing, you about to be proved wrong. Now bring yo ass over here." I kept low to the ground and pointed the gun toward his crotch. "I'll blow yo dick right off you."

"Okay, okay." He slowly walked over to where I was on the side of the gas station.

When he got to me, I punched right in the mouth, and slipped behind him. Wrapping my arms around his neck, I put him in a sleeper hold and locked it in with all my might. It didn't take long for his legs to give out under him. He wobbled to the ground. I picked him up and threw him inside of the garbage can just as Princess pulled up on the side of me.

"Come on, daddy. Let's get the fuck out of here."

Chapter 14

When we pulled up in front of Rex's project buildings, he was standing on the sidewalk in a big ass puffy coat. The snow started to come down in big patches. The wind picked up, and it was so cold that as soon as we opened the door to the car, I damn near froze.

"Yo, I heard about what happened with the fam through TT. That shit fucked up. But my niggas ready to take that trip whenever y'all need us. I ain't wit mafuckas gettin' at my bloodline without it bein' some sort of repercussions."

"Cuz, we been chasin' this nigga for months now. He slippery as a floor saturated with baby oil. I mean, every time we get close to him, somethin' happens in his favor. Now he got our daughter and mother, after killin' our siblings."

Rex pulled out a fat ass blunt, and sparked it. He inhaled deeply. "Yo, where that nigga from anyway?"

I turned around in my seat to face him. "He from Chicago, but his stompin' grounds is in Memphis, mostly Orange Mound now. He plugged wit some Blood niggas out of New Orleans. They all do that heroin shit, so they got this dope fiend shit in common."

Rex handed the blunt to me and I inhaled it deeply. "Cuz, what you need from me right now?" he asked Princess, sipping from a bottle of Hennessy.

"Well first things first, I need you to take this Corvette and give us another whip that ain't hot 'cuz we just jacked a nigga for this one like an hour ago. Then, we need two pistols, and we'll be able to make it back home. We gotta get out of New York before we wind up in prison out here. We already got too much shit goin' on in Tennessee as it is. The last thing we need is to get popped off up here," Princess said, taking the blunt away from me and pulling on it. She inhaled it hard, and blew the smoke out.

"Well, that ain't askin' for much. I can make that happen. Y'all stay right here." He jumped out of the car.

I watched him run into the project building. Princess grabbed my thigh and squeezed it. "You okay, baby?"

I laid all the way back in my seat and closed my eyes. I was exhausted. I wanted to get somewhere and lay down. It had been so long since we had been able to enjoy a full night of uninterrupted sleep. My body was tired and I could feel it. "Baby, I'm good I'm just tired. I'm ready for us to be able to rest."

She yawned. "I know, baby, me too. I'm tired of all this rippin' and runnin' that we gotta do every single day. I just want us to get our baby back so that we can live happily ever after."

"Happily ever after. Just think about that for a second. Don't you understand that we'll never be able to live happily ever after no more?" I sat up and shook my head. "Princess, we got all kinds of mafuckas lookin' for us right now. Police, niggas in the hood, our family, everybody. Ain't too many places we can go. And closin' our eyes even to blink now is dangerous. This shit is really real, ma."

She stretched her arms over her head. "Yeah, you right. But at least we in this shit together. That's all that matters to me. As long as I got you, don't nothin' else matter to me. You're my everything, so until they bury us, I'm gon' be ridin' right beside you bustin' my gun."

Rex jogged over to the car and got in the backseat. "Yo, here go two .40 Calibers. These mafuckas a knock a nigga head clean off his shoulders. Here go two clips a piece. My man's finna pull up in this lil' Lincoln Town Car, too. Now it ain't as flashy as this one, but it'll get y'all back home and it get good gas mileage."

As if on cue, a dark blue Lincoln Town Car pulled up behind us and a fat dude got out with some short dreads. He had a half of ski mask over his face, and a big puffy blue coat. When Rex saw him, he got out of the car, they embraced.

"Yo, these my people right here. They good."

"This the joint right here that you was tellin' me about. This the Vette?" he asked, speaking of the Corvette that we were sitting in.

"Yeah, this it," Rex said, pulling his collar up, shielding his ears from the harsh winter winds.

"Yo, what they tryna get from me for this? I'll give up no more than ten gees for it." He ran his hand across the hood of the car.

Rex held out his hand. "Since it's you, just give me eight. I'm lettin' you know now, this mafucka is hot. So, don't think you buyin' a brand-new ass whip for ten bands and ain't no karma come wit it. They just jacked this mafucka like an hour ago. It's best you get it to yo shop right away."

The fat nigga went into his pants pocket and pulled out a knot of money. He handed Rex a bundle. "Yo, that's an even ten. I don't take handouts, my nigga, and I ain't in the business of owin' nobody shit. Far as what you advisin' I do wit it, I got this. Y'all get out of my whip so I can do my thing. Time is money, my nigga, and y'all slow in' me down."

Rex walked up on him and got in his face. "Yo, hold on wit how you talkin' to them, boss. This ain't that."

The fat nigga bumped him out of his face. “Yo, you ain’t bout that life, Rex. Stop flexin’ in front of yo people before I have to embarrass you. Word is bond.” He opened the driver’s door, and Princess damn near fell out.

“Damn, nigga, it ain’t that serious. I damn near busted my shit fuckin’ wit you.”

I opened the passenger’s door, jumped out the whip, and ran up on him, putting that big ass .40 caliber against his forehead and pressing it hard. “You bitch ass nigga, I don’t know who the fuck you think you is, but if you ever hurt my baby girl again, I’ll blow yo muthafuckin head off. That’s my word. You got that? “

He looked up at me like he wasn’t fazed. “Nigga, if you any kin to Rex, I ain’t worried about you pullin’ that trigger. But it’s in yo best interest to get that gun from up against my head, or shit about to get real ugly for you, homie. That’s my word.”

Princess stepped out of the car. “What you tryna say? You sayin’ that whoever got my cousin blood ain’t about that life or somethin’?”

He frowned his face, and curled his upper lip. “Nigga, get that gun out of my face so I can be on my way.” He reached up to knock it out of his face, and that’s when I busted.

Boo-yah!

I knocked his noodles all over the snow in the street. Princess stood over him and busted three times, making his body hop and jump in the street.

“Fuck nigga, you ain’t know death was loomin’ on yo punk ass, did you?”

Rex reached down and went into his pockets, pulling out a fat ass cartoon type knot of money. “I knew one day that that nigga mouth was gon' get him in trouble. He just can't never keep that mafucka closed."

"Where you know this nigga from anyway, Rex?" Princess asked, sitting behind the wheel of the Lincoln Town Car. When she opened the door, the lights came on in the interior. She looked over the inside of the car.

"That's my second cousin on my father side. I guess he thought that since we was related, I wasn't gon' let shit happen to 'em. It's been a few times that the homies wanted to get up wit his glamour, but they gave him a G-pass on account of me. Quiet as kept, if y'all wasn't about to blow that nigga shit back, then I was." He snatched a chain from his neck and stomped him in the stomach.

I slid in beside Princess in the Lincoln. I felt like it was time to get out of New York city. I ain't really know nothing about the niggas out there, and the last thing I needed to happen was for me to be locked up in a state where I wasn't plugged wit nobody. That always spelled disaster. At least in the state of Illinois, or Tennessee I had a little knowledge about what was what. I could navigate a little bit. I mean, not that I was ready to go to prison or nothing, because I planned on holding court in the streets. I was sure that Princess was down with that plan. It just all depended on what was good with our daughter.

Before we could say our goodbyes to Rex, some female walked up to him and smacked the shit out of him. "I can't believe you got my sister pregnant, too. Now what the fuck we gon' do wit both of us bein' pregnant by yo careless ass?" she tried to swing on him again but he ducked.

"Yo, chill the fuck out. It's too cold out here for that shit." He jogged a little bit, trying to get away from her and she actually had the nerve to try and chase him. I was wondering why she ain't see that dead body in the street, or maybe she did and just didn't give a fuck because him having her sister pregnant was more devastating to her at the end of the day.

Princess opened the car door, and stepped into the snow. "Uh, excuse you, but can you stop chasin' my cousin around the damn street like you crazy or somethin'?"

By that time, the female had caught him and was slapping him on the back while he tried to get her off of him. "How you gon' have me and my sister pregnant? Do you have any idea how humiliatin' that is? Our kids gonna be fuckin' brother and sister, and cousins at the same time. What kind of shit is that?" She tried to throw him down, but he was too strong to allow that to happen.

Princess ran up on the girl and pulled her down by her hair, slamming her to the ground so hard that her head bounced off the curb, and split open. Before the girl could get a chance to recover, Princess straddled her and started beating her across the face with the handle of her gun. "Bitch. You. Gone. Act. Like. You. Didn't. Hear. Me. Tell. You. To. Leave. My. Cousin. The. Fuck. Alone. Now. Die. Bitch. Die," she said as she beat her over the head again and again until there was a big puddle of red snow in the street.

I got out and pulled Princess off the girl when I saw her turn the gun around, ready to bust. "Baby, get yo ass up and get in the car. Damn, we got enough heat out here," I said, picking her up and carrying her.

Rex stood, looking down at his baby's mother with his eyes wide open. He looked sick. He walked over to where she lay in a puddle of blood and dropped to his knees. "Damn, cuz. You ain't have to do her like that. I actually cared about this girl. Now look at her."

Her head was wide open with blood pouring from it like a pitcher of Kool-Aid. Her mouth was wide open, and her jaw was twisted the wrong way. He held her in his arms, and it blew my mind when he started crying. "Damn, cuz, you just kilt my bitch. You kilt my daughter's mama. I'll never forgive you for this."

I was on my way to getting in the car beside Princess when I heard him say that, and that made me turn around and kneel down beside him. "Yo, she meant that much to you?"

He nodded. "This was my first love. The first piece of pussy that I had ever gotten. Yo, this shit should have never went down like this. Princess, you outta yo muthafuckin' mind ma. This shit ain't cool."

I looked over at Princess, and she turned her head to the side like she couldn't believe what she was hearing. I could tell that her mind was blown. "What?"

"You heard me. You ain't have to do her like this. Now what the fuck I'mma do? Who gon' raise our daughter?"

I got to looking around and was thankful that it was so much snow coming down. It looked like we were in some kind of a blizzard, with the wind blowing so hard that it made it hard for me to stand still. I felt the butterflies enter my stomach.

Princess got up out of the car and slammed the door. "What you just say?"

Before she could even get to him. *Boo-yah! Boo-yah!* His brains splashed across his dead baby mother and my Timbs.

Chapter 15

Princess woke me up in the middle of the night a week later by pushing on my chest. “Taurus, wake up. I can’t take this shit no more.” She had tears in her eyes, and her .45 pointed to her head.

I jerked up and got ready to take the gun away from her. But she jumped off the bed and put her back against the wall with the gun stuck under her chin.

“I swear to God, if you try and take this gun away from me right now, Taurus, I’m gon’ pull the trigger. I just need for you to hear me out right now because I am very vulnerable, and I don’t want to live no more.” Tears dropped from her cheeks and on to her chin.

“Baby, what’s the matter?” I asked, getting out of the bed and approaching her. The last thing I wanted for her to do was to pull that trigger. I knew that I needed her and I didn’t want to be the cause of her ending her own life, and my life in the process because she had become my whole entire world.

She shook her head. “I don’t know. But I feel very weak. I don’t think I can keep on pressin’ on without our daughter. I don’t know what that sicko is doin’ to her, and it’s drivin’ me crazy. And then on top of that, I don’t want us havin’ to look over our shoulders at all times. I’m just tired, Taurus.” She slid down the wall and kept the gun pressed to her head.

I sank down to my knees and slowly made my way across the floor toward her. “Baby, I’m not gonna take the gun away, but can I at least hold you because you need me right now?” I asked with my voice as calm as possible.

She shrugged her shoulders. “I don’t know.” She lowered the gun and dropped it on the floor, breaking down into a fit of sobs. "I miss our baby so much, daddy. I think about her all the time. I wonder what that sicko is doin' to our baby and if she's even still alive. The dreams are startin' to wear me out."

I crawled across the floor and wrapped her into my arms. As soon as her head hit my chest, she broke down and let her tears fly. "It's okay, baby. I'm here and I understand because I'm feelin' the same level of pain. That's our baby together and she means so much to the both of us. Right now, you're feelin' like you failed as a mother and a protector, and I'm feelin' the same way as a father. But what you have to understand is that we aren't dealin' with an average situation that most parents ever have to go through or deal with. We have a lunatic on our hands, and we can't allow for him to break us down to the point we start to give up on ourselves or our little girl. You puttin' that gun to your head is equivalent to Juice doin' it to you. Now, you're my baby girl and I know that you are way more stronger than that. You're the strongest person I have ever known."

"I know, baby, but it is so hard." She grabbed my wife beater and smashed her face into my chest, sobbing uncontrollably. I could feel her body shaking. "I don't know how you mask it all because it is breakin' me down more than anything in my entire life."

I took a deep breath and kissed her on the top of her head. "We gon' get through this shit together, Princess. You and me. We been through so much that we cannot let this nigga break us. We are all that we have, don't you understand that? If you pull that trigger, then I'mma blow my shit back, too, because I ain't livin' in this world without you. But where does that leave Jahliya? Who gonna save her then?" I felt the tears coming down my cheeks. "Your life ain't just about you no more,

Princess. Everything that you do now, you gotta factor in how it's gonna affect me and our daughter. I can't be in this life without you. You're my everything."

She wrapper her arms around me and started crying harder than I had ever felt her cry before. "I know, daddy, and I love you so fuckin' much. I don't want to hurt you or our daughter but I've just been feelin' so fuckin' weak lately."

"Well I'm gon' sit right here and cry with you all night, until you feel better and know that you are not alone. Yo daddy is right here and I will never leave your side."

I wound up holding her for a full three hours that night. She broke down so much that I literally started to worry about her. I knew that she had been through a lot and we had caused a whole lot of trouble. I didn't know how many bodies Princess had under her belt before we started our spree, but I knew that now she had a bunch. After a while, that starts to pick at your mind. The souls of the lives you took actually haunt you, and mentally, it gets real rough.

I was dealing with my own issues of nightmares, waking up in cold sweats, and my appetite was nonexistent. I really missed my daughter. I missed my mother as well, and I wondered how she was doing, and if our daughter was safe and sound.

***

Then it happened. About two weeks after we got back from New York, my mother hit up my phone. "Baby I'm at the Greyhound bus station right outside of Jackson. I need for you to come and get me. I don't have any money, and I just escaped from Juice. He's been rapin' me so much, baby, that

I had to leave or he was gonna kill me," she screamed into the phone.

"Ma, where is Jahliya?"

"She still with him. When I left, she was in the arms of one of those little girls that be walkin' around his house all naked and stuff."

The first thing I did was silently thank God that my daughter was still alive. I personally thought that Juice had already killed our little girl on some spiteful shit. But then again, he was the type that whenever he did something he had to brag about it, so I guess I was waiting on that phone call more than anything else.

Princess jumped up and grabbed the phone. "Was my baby healthy when you left? Like, has he been feedin' her every day? Tell me somethin', please," Princess whined.

"Please, y'all, just come get me and I'll tell you everything that you need to know."

***

Four hours later, she was in the car, spilling the beans about everything that Juice had been doing to her and our daughter.

"Your brother is sick, Taurus. As soon as he got me to that house of his, he ain't waste no time rapin' me in front of his little girlfriend, and she seemed like she was with that shit, too. He choked me until I passed out and did his thing to me while he held a gun to my head. He treated me way worse than your father ever had, and I don't know what I did to him in life to make him do all of that to me." She placed her hands over her face and broke down crying.

Princess shook her head. “That’s fucked up. I mean, how can a person do all of that to their own mother?”

I looked into my rearview mirror and made eye contact with her. It’s okay, mama, you safe now. I’ll never let that nigga hurt you again as long as I’m alive,” I promised, meaning every word that I spoke to her.

“What is he plannin’ on doin’ with our daughter? Did he say?” Princess asked, turned all the way around in her seat.

My mother shook her head. “I don’t know, but when I left, he was makin’ her call him daddy. That boy was kissin’ all over her like he was the father.”

Out of everything that she had told us, including the rapes, hearing that pissed me off the most, so bad that I couldn’t see clearly. I got to imagining Jahliya calling him daddy and I felt like killing something. I actually got to seeing red.

Princess curled up her lip. “And what was his girl doin’ the entire time?”

“She was makin’ it seem like she was her mother. I’m sorry, baby.”

Princess turned around and plopped down in her seat. “I’mma kill that nigga, and that bitch. Didn’t nobody lay in that hospital bed for fourteen hours in labor with her but me. She ain’t s’posed to call no female mama, if it ain’t me. I can’t wait to get my hands on them.”

“Ma, where exactly is he stayin’? Did he move you to more than one location?”

She nodded. “Yeah, baby, we didn’t stay in no place for more than two nights. That boy constantly movin’ because he know that the whole world is after him. Every time we was drivin’ somewhere, somebody was shootin’ at the car. It got to the point that when I rolled with him, I just stayed down in the back seat from fear of bein' hit by a bullet."

"What type of security he got wit him at all times?" I asked, trying to assess the situation. I needed to know how he was rolling around so I could know how to penetrate his circle and knock some of their heads off. I didn't care what I had to do, I was going to find him and get my daughter out of his care. The fact that she was being forced to call him daddy was driving me crazy. Not to mention, I could also see how bad it was affecting Princess.

"He gettin' followed around by his Bloodz. They be rollin' behind him in a brown or all-black van. It's about ten of them in it, and they all got plenty of guns and ammunition. Trust me, I seen them loadin' it up one day and it didn't look pretty." She broke down. "I don't understand why he turned out the way that he did. Yo father messed him up and it ain't no comin' back from that. I done lost all of my children to the streets, and it shouldn't be like that. I've been a good girl my entire life."

"Ma, it ain't got nothin' to do with you. It's just the sins of our family all together, startin' with our father."

I didn't know how to explain things to my mother to get her to understand that it wasn't her fault, because I didn't have all the answers myself. All I knew was that I had to kill Juice once and for all. It would be the only way that we could go on living without having to worry about being blindsided and murdered in cold blood.

"Well for now, we gon' put you up in a nice hotel, and you gon' have to stay there for a few weeks, or until we squash this stuff with Juice, because it ain't safe.," Princess said kissing her gun that she had pulled from under the seat of the car.

"Man, I can't wait to knock his brains out of his head. It's gonna be the best thing that ever happened to me besides you, Taurus." She smiled and winked at me.

We put my mother up at the Waldorf Astoria, and hit the road. We'd decided that we were going to find Juice and it didn't matter if it took us an entire month to do so. We were prepared to live out of the car for the whole time. He had to be killed and we had to get our daughter back. My mother had told me all the spots that she'd visited with Juice and we'd written them all down and planned on hitting them all up until we found out where he was and where he was keeping Jahliya. I was hungrier than three slaves working, but tired of seeing Princess break down over our daughter. I knew that over time it would take a toll on her.

"Daddy, you know what?" she said as we hit the freeway, on our way to the first location.

"What's that, baby?" I asked, stuffing some French fries into my mouth.

"I wanna torture that nigga in the worst way imaginable. I mean, just think about all the damage that he done caused all by himself. This nigga done put us through so much that we owe it to him to torture him worse than we have ever tortured anybody. I mean, on some real shit. You remember how you told Donnell that if he ever came near me again, you would cut him up and make me eat him, just so I could shit him in the toilet later on?"

I nodded. I'd meant every word of that. The last thing I wanted was for him to come near my Princess ever again. She was officially my baby girl, and I was willing to kill Donnell's punk ass over that.

"Well, when we find Juice, I want us to eat him after we chop him into lil' bitty pieces. I mean, I'm talkin' about usin' hot sauce and everything. I wanna enjoy this nigga like I have never enjoyed a meal before. Do you think we can do that?" she asked, looking at me from the passenger's seat.

I couldn't help laughing because she was so serious. I mean, you could tell by the expression on her face that she was not kidding. Juice had caused her so much pain, and the only way I guess she felt she could get over him was if she murdered him by torture and then ate every piece of him. "Yeah, we can do that, baby. I'm thinkin' lightin' candles and makin' a whole romantic night of it. He can be our main course, then we can fuck on a full stomach, passin' gas and all types of shit. I'm cool wit that."

She busted up laughing. "Daddy, I know you just cracked a joke, but I'm serious as hell."

"Me, too, ma."

We were just pulling out of the rest stop right outside of Nashville when my phone vibrated, and Hood Rich's face came across the screen. I put him on speakerphone. "What's good, Hood Rich?"

"I need to meet up wit you so we can talk business. it's very important."

"Yo, that sounds good, but right now I'm goin' through some real-life shit in search of my daughter. A muhfucka done kidnapped her and I gotta get her back before they take her life."

"That's what I wanna talk to you about. I think I got some information that a be very useful to you. Where can we meet?"

He picked me and Princess up in a helicopter three hours later in Nashville, Tennessee. It was already extremely windy, and since we had not been eating that much, me and Princess had lost a lot of weight. I think I might have lost like ten pounds, and she had to be down to about 110. So, as we ran to get into the helicopter, the wind was throwing my baby girl around.

It looked like she was having a real tough time making it to the chopper, and that broke my heart because I knew that she was stressing worse than she ever had before. We had to put a pin in the whole Juice thing, and we had to get our daughter back.

I had to help her to get into the chopper. When I picked her up into it, I could feel that she was way lighter than I had ever remembered her being before.

When we got in, I wrapped my arms around her protectively and kissed her on the cheek. "I promise you, ma, we gon' find this nigga and I'mma let you eat him for dinner. We gon' do that shit together, the way it's s'posed to go."

She laid her head on my shoulder. "I believe you, daddy. I love you so freakin' much. I don't know what I would do without you."

We wound up at Hood Rich's big mansion in Austin, Texas. It was huge, and very luxurious. When I first walked through the double doors, I couldn't even breathe because I was holding my breath. I didn't even know that I was doing it. I stepped onto marble floors that squeaked at every little step. He had a statue of himself in the center of the big living room as soon as you came through the big doors with a grand piano to the left of it. The mansion was well furnished, and everything looked brand new. Even though we didn't go in that direction, I could see a big pool in the backyard that had water so blue it looked like mouthwash.

Hood Rich led us down the stairs, and into a big den that had a projector screen in it, and a long table. "Would you like anything to drink?" he asked as a maid came into the room wearing a uniform that looked two sizes too small for her. She looked full blooded Mexican, and had a big ol' round booty.

"Nah, we good. Yo, you said you had some information in regards to my daughter. What's good?" Princess said, crossing her fingers and placing them on the table. She gave him her undivided attention, and so did I.

He laughed. "I like her, Taurus. She wanna get straight to the point. Lil' mama, that's just how I am, so let me get on wit it." He curled up his upper lip. "That nigga Meech out for blood. He just tried to kill me in our homeland, after makin' a deal with the Jewish outfit. I guess they want me dead and they gon' put him in charge of the organization that I built from the ground up. It's millions and millions of dollars involved, and this shit stretches all the way to Russia."

Princess squinted her eyes. "Yo, no disrespect, but what that got to do with us?"

"Yeah, Hood Rich, I'm not followin' you. I know you got plenty mafuckas that can handle Meech for you. Everybody know he was eatin' off you and your Mob."

Hood Rich nodded. "That's just it, this thing is bigger than me and my mob. As I said before, it stretches all the way to Russia. Do you remember Nastia?"

I nodded, "Yeah, I remember her. What about her?"

"I need for you to find her for me, and bring her here, or just bring me her head. I will take either one. I know that she trusts you over everybody else. There is a wager that's been placed on her head, specifically to me, and if I can serve her head on a platter, then I can break into Russia. I also gotta knock off Meech, but I'm sure I can handle that. After all, I did make him."

I shook my head. "Once again, you said that you had information on my daughter, but you ain't said nothin' about her. You're just talkin' about your problems." I was starting to get heated because I felt we were wasting valuable time sitting there in front of him when we could have been out there looking for Juice and Jahliya.

He grunted and shook his head. Looking over his shoulders, he snapped his finger at his big beefy guard, and the man walked out of the room, waving us to follow him.

We walked two rooms over and into a closet, where the big beefy man opened the door and then moved the clothes that were hanging there out of the way. After he did that, it exposed a big steel door that looked almost like a safe. It had a latch on it that he turned to his left again and again until it opened. When it did, we followed him into a long dark hallway that got colder the further we got into it, it also felt damp. We must've been walking for close to two minutes before we stepped on to concrete, and in the distance, I could see the lights of a fire.

"Never doubt me, Taurus. Make sure you teach yo woman that, as well."

As we got further into the dungeon, I looked ahead, and a big ass smile came across my face.

"Holy shit, I know that ain't," Princess hollered and took off running. "We got yo ass now, nigga. Taurus, I don't give a fuck what deal he tryna make wit you, we doin' that shit."

I nodded at her as tears sailed down my cheeks. My heart was thumping so hard in my chest, as I watched Princess run up to Juice, who was chained to the wall of Hood Rich's dungeon, ass naked with a red ball gag in his mouth.

Soon as she got to him, she took a crazy bite out of his chest and ran her nails across his face, leaving four long scratches. "I hate chu, Juice! You ruined my life! Where's my daughter?" She grabbed the ball out of his mouth and back handed him with all of her might.

Juice spit blood across the brick wall and started laughing as it dripped from his mouth. "Fuck you, bitch! Fuck you and that turncoat ova there!" he laughed like a maniac.

Princess looked over her shoulder at me with tears in her eyes. "Let's kill this nigga, Taurus, please, I'm beggin' you. You promised me that we would. I hate this nigga and he's destryoin' me." She dropped to her knees with her face in her lap, while Juice continued to laugh behind her.

"You stupid bitch, when I get out of here, I'm killin' you and that bitch nigga! Beware of that red rag. Beware of them hittas!" he laughed again before coughing up a bloody loogey.

Hood Rich tapped me on my shoulder and nodded toward the door that we came through. If the tears weren't comin down before, now I completely broke down as I saw the same maid from before, walking toward us with Jahliya in her arms. My bi-polar kicked in right away because there were tears streaming down my cheeks, but a big smile on my face.

Hood Rich handed be a big ass knife with sharp ridges. It gleamed in the dark dungeon and everything that I had been through with Juice ran rapid in my mind like a short movie. I thought about that nigga raping my mother, killing my sister, and putting his filthy hands on my daughter. That made the tears come down my face even harder because she was precious, and it was my job to protect her, period. But even with all of that shit killing me, nothing hurt me more than to see Princess on her knees, rocking back and forth lost deep within her own mind. I could only imagine, her slowly having a nervous breakdown. I ran over to her and kneeled beside her, before pulling her up. "Baby, look behind you. Hood Rich got her back for us."

She turned around and her eyes got as big as saucers. I expected her to run over to our daughter after worrying about her for so long, but she did none of that. Instead she pointed at the maid, "Is she sleeping?" The maid nodded *yes* and continued to bounce Jahliya up and down on her hip. "Well, good, step back into that door 'cause I don't want her seein' this," Princess calmly directed.

I watched as the lady followed Princess' orders. As soon as she disappeared, I walked up to Juice with a heart as cold as ice. He was a mortal and no longer my brother. I hated that nigga. *This bully. This rapist. This demon.*

His weak ass knew that this was the moment of truth, and now that it was time for him to reap what he had sown, all of the bitch came out of him.

"Taurus! Taurus! I'm still yo brother, nigga! Ay! Don't do this shit. Don't!" he pled.

I chuckled and then I gave the knife to Princess, "Ladies first, lil' momma."

She took the knife and turned to Juice. She spoke with a coldness I'd never heard before. "You played me, Juice. You played me like a fuckin' fool. You killed my brother, my aunty and you put yo filthy ass hands on my daughter! You took what was beautiful in me and turned it into somethin' hideous and ugly like yo callous ass. You gotta pay for that!"

Princess raised the knife over her head and brought it down with unrelenting force.

Thwack!

The sharpness slashed across his face, opening a huge, ugly gash down his cheek.

Juice cried out in pain and begged for mercy, something he had never shown his victims. Princess shook her head *no* emphatically. "No mercy for you, you heartless bastard!" She slashed him across the face again and again, causing blood to spray up into the air.

"*Ahhhhhhh*! Taurus, stop this shit! *Pleeeaseeee*! Somebody stop this crazy bitch!" he screamed.

"*Crazy*? Trust me, behind every *crazy* bitch is a fuck nigga that made her that way. I hate men like you. Y'all take advantage of defenseless women. Y'all violate kids and ruin families. You had no right doin' what you did to us!" She slashed the knife across his face again, splitting his cheek wide open, so deep that I could see his bone, before she slammed the knife into his shoulder and stepping behind me. "Kill this bitch nigga, Taurus. As much as I want to, I know it ain't my place." She wiped Juice's blood from her forehead, stepped on her tippy toes and planted a soft kiss on my cheek.

I stepped forward and eyed him with extreme hatred. I saw my life flash before my eyes: all of the injustices niggas like Juice and my father inflicted. I saw my father beating my mother, right before he killed our uncle in front of us. I saw Juice whooping my ass in the backyard, then me knocking him out in our bedroom a few nights later.

I saw Gotto's death. I saw Shakia committing suicide. I saw Shanetta getting shot. Then the hacking of parts of Tremarion. One by one, all of the murders started to go through my head at once. I saw Tywain's face in his casket, and a tear dropped from my eye. Juice had been responsible for his death. I blinked and the tears came down full bore. The next thing I knew, I snapped.

I snatched the big knife out of Juice's shoulder and slammed it back into the same hole before yanking it out and slicing him over and over again. In my mind's eye, he switched back and forth from being my father to meeting himself.

You look too much like that nigga. You acted too much like him.

They were one in the same. They had both hurt my mother and sister. They were evil.

Slash after slash, I went crazy. "Nigga you raped our mother." *Slash.* "The same woman that gave yo bitch ass life." *Slash.* "You killed our only sister, when yo job was to protect her." *Slash.* "And you put yo…" *Slash.* "Nasty ass hands…" *Slash.* "On my daughter." *Slash.* "You daddy, tho', huh?" *Slash.* "Nahhh, fuck nigga!" *Slash.* "I'm her muhfuckin' father!" *Slash.* "That's ma mufuckin' seed!" I went crazy until I felt Princess shaking me and pulling me backward. Only then, did I come out of my foggy haze.

"Taurus! Taurus! It's over, baby. You fucked that nigga up! Look at him!" she hollered, pointing with her head, wrapping her arms around me.

Juice was slumped over as if he'd had all that he could take. Blood continued to drip from his face. He had open gashes all over it. He looked like he had been attacked by a million cats at once. His chest heaved up and down as if he was getting ready to have an asthma attack.

He slowly turned his face toward me and Princess. He looked like he was in extreme pain. He blinked, swallowed and then tried to spit, but his lip was split in two. The loogey dripped through the crack and ran down his chin. Juice continued to breathe, his chest rising and falling and then out of nowhere he started laughing like a maniac. "Ahhhhhhh! Fuck you! I'm waitin' on you, nigga. Kill me like I killed Mary." He coughed and laughed simultaneously.

I imagined my little sister's face and before I could stop myself, I raised the knife over my head and ran to him, "Arrggghhh!" I slammed it directly into his heart, grabbed his throat and with the handle of knife, I lifted him in the air as far as the chains would allow, holding him there. I could feel his body shake and tremble as he coughed up blood. I held him there until my arm gave out. I fell to the floor in front of his bloody and leaking body.

Princess crawled over to me and wrapped her arms around my shoulder "It's over, daddy. That bitch nigga finally dead. Now we can focus on somethin' else."

My chest heaved up and down. I missed my daughter. I wanted to hold her in my arms so bad. I helped Princess come to a standing position before looking Juice over one last time. I felt weak *and* strong. I felt like he was a sacrifice for all of the sins of our family's past. With the knife still lodged in his chest, I kissed Princess on the forehead. "You know what, baby?"

She looked up at me with exhaustion on her face "What's that, daddy?"

I took one last look at Juice. "My pops always said that one of us would kill the other."

Juice must've forgotten that even though I had a heart and a whole lot of common decency, like him, I was RAISED AS A GOON, I thought as I looked around for a rag to wipe his blood off of me. Then, and only then, could I begin a new chapter in my life.

THE END

R.I.P JUICE, SHAKIA, SHANETTA, GOTTO, TY-WAIN

Stay Connected with Us!

Text **LOCKDOWN** to 22828 to stay up-to-date with new releases, sneak peaks, contests and more…

Thank you!

Coming Soon from Lock Down Publications/Ca$h Presents

BOW DOWN TO MY GANGSTA

By **Ca$h & Jamaica**

TORN BETWEEN TWO

By **Coffee**

BLOOD OF A BOSS **IV**

By **Askari**

BRIDE OF A HUSTLA **III**

THE FETTI GIRLS **III**

By **Destiny Skai**

WHEN A GOOD GIRL GOES BAD **II**

By **Adrienne**

LOVE & CHASIN' PAPER **II**

By **Qay Crockett**

THE HEART OF A GANGSTA **II**

By **Jerry Jackson**

TO DIE IN VAIN **II**

By **ASAD**

LOYAL TO THE GAME **IV**

By **T.J. & Jelissa**

A DOPEBOY'S PRAYER **II**

By **Eddie "Wolf" Lee**

A HUSTLER'S DECEIT **III**

THE BOSS MAN'S DAUGHTERS **III**

BAE BELONGS TO ME **II**

By **Aryanna**

TRUE SAVAGE **III**

By **Chris Green**

IF LOVING YOU IS WRONG…

By **Jelissa**

BLOODY COMMAS **II**

By **T.J. Edwards**

Available Now

(CLICK TO PURCHASE)

RESTRAINING ORDER **I & II**

By **CA$H & Coffee**

LOVE KNOWS NO BOUNDARIES **I II & III**

By **Coffee**

RAISED AS A GOON I & II

By **Ghost**

LAY IT DOWN **I & II**

LAST OF A DYING BREED

By **Jamaica**

LOYAL TO THE GAME

LOYAL TO THE GAME II

LOYAL TO THE GAME III

By **TJ & Jelissa**

PUSH IT TO THE LIMIT

By **Bre' Hayes**

BLOOD OF A BOSS **I II & III**

By **Askari**

THE STREETS BLEED MURDER **I, II & III**

THE HEART OF A GANGSTA

By **Jerry Jackson**

CUM FOR ME

CUM FOR ME 2

CUM FOR ME 3

An **LDP Erotica Collaboration**

BRIDE OF A HUSTLA **I & II**

THE FETTI GIRLS **I & II**

By **Destiny Skai**

WHEN A GOOD GIRL GOES BAD

By **Adrienne**

A GANGSTER'S REVENGE **I II III & IV**

THE BOSS MAN'S DAUGHTERS

THE BOSS MAN'S DAUGHTERS II

A SAVAGE LOVE **I & II**

BAE BELONGS TO ME

A HUSTLER'S DECEIT I, II

By **Aryanna**

A KINGPIN'S AMBITON

A KINGPIN'S AMBITION **II**

I MURDER FOR THE DOUGH

By **Ambitious**

TRUE SAVAGE

TRUE SAVAGE II

By **Chris Green**

A DOPEBOY'S PRAYER

By **Eddie "Wolf" Lee**

WHAT ABOUT US **I & II**

NEVER LOVE AGAIN

THUG ADDICTION

By **Kim Kaye**

THE KING CARTEL **I, II & III**

By **Frank Gresham**

THESE NIGGAS AIN'T LOYAL **I, II & III**

By **Nikki Tee**

GANGSTA SHYT **I II &III**

By **CATO**

THE ULTIMATE BETRAYAL

By **Phoenix**

BOSS'N UP **I & II**

By **Royal Nicole**

I LOVE YOU TO DEATH

By Destiny J

I RIDE FOR MY HITTA

I STILL RIDE FOR MY HITTA

By **Misty Holt**

LOVE & CHASIN' PAPER

By **Qay Crockett**

TO DIE IN VAIN

By **ASAD**

BOOKS BY LDP'S CEO, CA$H

(CLICK TO PURCHASE)

TRUST IN NO MAN

TRUST IN NO MAN 2

TRUST IN NO MAN 3

BONDED BY BLOOD

SHORTY GOT A THUG

THUGS CRY

THUGS CRY 2

THUGS CRY 3

TRUST NO BITCH

TRUST NO BITCH 2

TRUST NO BITCH 3

TIL MY CASKET DROPS

RESTRAINING ORDER

RESTRAINING ORDER 2

IN LOVE WITH A CONVICT

Coming Soon

BONDED BY BLOOD 2

BOW DOWN TO MY GANGSTA

Made in the USA
Monee, IL
15 November 2024